A Harvest of Broken Stars by Ole Åsli and Tony Bakkejord

A *Starfall* Novel

ISBN: 978-82-93794-99-8 (ebook)

Authors' website: www.tokonger.no

Email: post@tokonger.no

Cover design by Ana Ristovska

www.anaristovska.com

Prologue

The frightened badger squealed, as Eldrick held it aloft by the scruff of its neck.

Roaring cheers from the audience in the arena above drowned out the cleric's chants and incantations.

From his deep pockets, he produced the black and purple starglass, just larger than his thumb. The crystal emitted a high-pitched hum, an audible hint of its inherent magical energies.

As his shrill voice rose to a crescendo, he drove the starglass into the badger's chest. Such bloodshed was not necessary for the ritual to work, but Eldrick felt a surge of satisfaction while the helpless animal trembled and the crystal absorbed its spirit.

While the small heart beat for the last time, the hum from the starglass changed, now slightly out of tune. The taint of the necromancy would distort the crystal and its magic as long as it lasted.

Eldrick winced as he briefly considered the cost of the ritual, but regained his composure by reminding himself of the benefits if the experiment succeeded.

He dropped the limp badger to the dungeon floor and moved over to the stone table, and the second part of the ritual.

The arena provided plenty of corpses, especially when the gladiatorial games coincided with the full moon festival.

Eldrick admired the muscular frame of the fallen combatant. He let his pale hand glide slowly over the blood-smeared skin as he performed the incantations of the animate dead spell. His fingers found the stab wound that had sealed his faith: a deep hole at the side of his neck. A proper gladiator's death, executed by a superior fighter.

With his left hand, the cleric inserted the starglass into the fatal wound and pushed it as deep in the broad chest as his fingers could reach. Satisfied, he put both hands palms down on the dead gladiator's torso and finished the ritual, combining the animated corpse with the badger's spirit trapped in the starglass.

'Rise,' Eldrick said.

The corpse obeyed, its movement slow and limbered. It stood, motionless and unblinking, as the cleric pressed his bloodied hands against its temples.

Eldrick did not utter a single word, instead conveying the commands of his quest spell as images until the undead shook as its muscles tightened.

The instructions were received, and the quest was accepted. Eldrick glanced over at the small table by the door. The hourglass showed that the whole ritual had taken him less than a quartermark.

Eldrick stepped to the side, and smiled as the fallen gladiator exited through the open cell door.

Chapter 1: Ice

Ada doubled over as cold claws shredded her from the inside. The visceral manifestation of abandonment, self-loathing and insecurity.

The sensation was all too familiar. Her flings and affairs often left her with a broken heart or a broken arm. She lingered overlong in foul relationships, allowing her partners to gnaw at her self-respect until there was nothing left. She would accept any treatment as long as she did not have to face the world alone.

Zac let her move in soon after they met. Or, rather, she never moved out after she spent the first night with him. Zac was a player in the prosperous herb industry. He could have been wealthy if he put more effort into marketing and selling the various herbs he cultured and imported, rather than smoking them. Ada spent some time selling his produce in the streets and taverns of Sandcastle, avoiding the watchful eyes of Sheriff Blackmane's guards.

Having spent most of her teens in the streets, Ada knew how to keep her partners satisfied. She would build them up with lavish praise and expertly care for their physical needs and desires.

A few days ago, she had done exactly that and left Zac dozing happily in bed as she went out to sell his wares.

This morning, her bedmate wept. Wet, poisonous tears of betrayal.

'I need to clear my conscience,' he said. And he did, at her expense. Much like he would have wiped up a puddle of vomit with her hair. Or her soul.

Why would anyone do that? Ada had been cheated on many times. And she pursued her own indiscretions. She understood. The admiration and expressions of love and desire from others might temporarily fill the void in those who were unable to love themselves. But she could never fathom why anyone would be so cruel as to confess their misdeeds to their partners, forcing upon them the unforgiving and irrevocable images of their beloved in steamy embraces with someone else.

The icy claws tore into her heart once again, forcing her to her knees. In the muddy street, images of Zac and his harlot flashed in her mind. She could have hated them both. But she was too overwhelmed with pain and fear to draw power from the dark energy of hatred.

Alone in the streets again, she had nobody to turn to for shelter, food or comfort. Her cold hands covered her face in a futile attempt to hold back the tears and stem the flood of thoughts and emotions. Covering her wild magic.

Slowly, a comforting sensation of warmth spread throughout her body. A weak tingling at first. Then gradually stronger, as if she was clutching a warm stone from the fireplace to her chest.

A barely audible *crack* made her look down between her fingers. Ice, thin as parchment, was forming on the mud around her legs. As her body sustained itself by channelling heat from her surroundings, the water on the ground froze. The patch of thin ice on this wet, autumn evening was plain for anyone to see. Revealing the presence of magic. Illegal magic.

Ada rose quickly, looking nervously around while stomping the ice back into the mud. Destroying the evidence of her abomination before anyone could notice and alert the sheriff's brutes.

The familiar feeling of shame enveloped Ada as she ran through the streets and alleys to get away from the crime scene. Shame, always shame. That's what they taught at the academy. She had spent three years in the custody of the wardens there, learning nothing but shame.

She understood now that every baby was born with talent. A vast potential for skills and abilities, minor or major. As the child grew, her environment, experiences, teaching and choices allowed some of those talents to develop. Skills not practised, abilities not used, potential not fulfilled, were peeled off. Pruned, much like a skilled gardener cut unwanted branches from a bush, directing it to grow into the desired size and form.

In another time, in a different place, this would be a natural process in any developing child. Not so here, not for Ada. For half a century, the aristocracy of Sandcastle had forced their savage methods upon any child showing the slightest affinity for magic. The children were taken from their families as soon as the affliction was apparent, some as young as four or five, and spent years of coercive pruning at the academy. Parents grieved as if their children had contracted a lethal disease or curse.

Magic was a weed, to be uprooted and cast away. Anyone caught *using* magic would be similarly disposed of.

In the eyes of the citizens of Sandcastle, Ada was a weed. Fortunately, she was not the only weed in this grand city.

Her flight brought her to the steps of the apothecary. Relieved, she brushed away white patches of ice from her wet clothes. Once again, she would seek sanctuary with her eccentric roommate from the academy. Rayn was always there when everyone else deserted her.

Chapter 2: Prison

One hundred and twenty-four steps, a turn left or right, and a walk of thirty beats. No doors, no locks. Except for the one on the cell door. So close. The chance will come. Has to come. With Owen on night duty, there will be no better opportunity. Not for a week. Owen, small and fat, hardly ever makes rounds. He stays in the guardroom playing cards. Losing at cards. If only I could get out that door.

Stop fooling yourself. Even twenty-four steps are too many. You would not make it. You are already dead.

Gilmir shook his head. Or rather, he thought he did, but the cold stone pressing against his left cheek told him otherwise. The left side of his body ached. He considered moving. Turning on the other side. On to his back? He braced his hand on the floor. Feeling the rotten straws against his bony fingers, he started pushing. The effort woke the slumbering pain. Pains. The stabbing from his missing fingernails. The burning from wounds across his back. They should have healed a long time ago. The dull throbbing in his head. He abandoned the plan.

For a moment, he wondered what was worse. The pain from the external world, or the voice in his internal realm, telling him to give up? Give in. Stop struggling. Just stop. He knew he could stop the voice, the suffering, the pain. End it all. Stop. Die.

A strange thought.

Gilmir shook his head. In the internal realm, at least. He went back to planning. Sustaining.

One hundred and twenty-four steps, 134 for Owen, 111 for the cruel Northman called Magnus, a turn and a walk of 20 beats. Give or take. The lock on the cell door is the only thing keeping me in. Maybe I have become so slim, I can slip through the bars?

He opened one eye to glance at the cell door. No. No living person was that thin. His head would not fit between the bars. Something flickered. There was movement outside the door. A small figure stalking across his field of vision. He closed his eyes again. It was of no consequence for him. Gilmir's heart skipped a beat, and then—*thump, thump, thump*. Quicker. Harder. His body was telling him something. He opened his eyes.

'Hey, halfling,' Gilmir said. Tried to say. It came out like a croak. Barely a whisper. The small silhouette kept moving. Slow and steady, without a sound. A staff in his hand. Some kind of scarf around his neck. A sliver of light fell over him. His wrists bore no shackles, but they had. The skin was red and chafed. *He is a prisoner. Moving. Free.* Gilmir had to stop him. It was almost too late. Already too late?

Do not fool yourself. Even if he opened the door and let you out, it would not help. You are as good as dead.

'Hey! Halfling! Stop!' This time, words came out. Like speech. The halfling turned. Put a finger to his lips and continued. *No, no, no! This is it. The one chance. The one I have been waiting for. Stop, you stupid little …* 'You are going the wrong way, you idiot.'

This time the little figure halted, and turned. He took four steps towards the bars. 'Keep quiet, man!' he hissed. 'What do you mean, the wrong way? You have ten beats to explain yourself.'

Gilmir got up on his elbow. His heart raced. 'I know the way out. The other way that is not through the guardroom with the five guards, and the sleeping quarters for the other ten. Which will take you to the stairs …'

'Tell me about the way I *should* take, then!'

'Let me out, and I'll show you.'

'Let you out? And … carry you? You are shaking, man! From the effort of keeping your head up.'

'One hundred and twenty-four steps. Help me with that, and I'll show you the way out. Afterwards, you can worry about yourself, and I'll worry about me.'

The halfling glanced left and right. He muttered something about his kind heart and the end of something. Coming to the door, he started picking the lock with something looking like needles. Gilmir braced himself for the effort, the pain, and the incredible challenge of getting to his feet. Inch by painstaking inch, he got to his feet. In time with the opening of the door. The halfling put his arm around Gilmir's waist and helped him make the first steps.

'How long have you been here?' the halfling asked, his tone incredulous.

'Two years, one hundred and sixty-seven days,' Gilmir answered between lumbering breaths.

Gilmir tipped his head to the left, in the opposite direction from where the halfling had been heading. To his credit, the halfling did not protest, stop or ask questions. They passed the other cells in silence. Someone whimpered from a cell, but the words were indiscernible. After about one hundred and twenty-four steps, they came to an intersection. Gilmir raised his head and pointed left. About twenty beats later, they found a hatch in the floor. The halfling opened the hatch and frowned.

'The sewer?'

'Yes.' The foul smell assaulted Gilmir's senses.

'Going where?'

'I have no idea.'

'You first, Stick Man.'

'That's Stick Elf to you,' Gilmir said and sat down, his feet dangling through the opening in the floor. With his hands on the edges, he planned to lower himself down before letting go. He did not get far before his feeble strength betrayed him.

He fell.

Chapter 3: Rayn

Rayn was a half-elf.

Elves rarely mated with humans. In fact, male elves never showed any interest in the plump and ephemeral beauty of human females. On rare occasions, a man would be so strong and valiant that he would be an acceptable mate for an elf female. Tall, beautiful and blessed with unnaturally long lives, such offspring would be esteemed in both cultures.

Far more common was the unsavoury union of men and elf females, invariably associated with warfare and raids. Their offspring would be shunned by men and elves alike, and most would be left to fend for themselves on the lowest rung of society as pickpockets, thieves and whores.

Rayn's mother chose a different path, raising her daughter alone in the woods for six years, until she died from starvation and exposure. Driven by hunger and unable to forage for food in winter, the orphan Rayn found her way to Sandcastle where her habit of talking to trees and stones had her apprehended and admitted to treatment at the academy within days of her arrival. By the time she met Ada, Rayn had spent more than three years subjected to magical desensitisation behind closed doors.

The off-set eyes she inherited from her father were the only distinguishing trait in an otherwise unremarkable visage. Rayn always seemed out of tune with other people, unable to comprehend their customs, rituals and social play-acting. Books and scrolls became her comfort, enabling her to share in the ideas, thoughts and emotions of other people without actually interacting with them.

Straight out of the academy, Rayn somehow managed to get an unpaid position as the apothecary's assistant. Despite her blunt demeanour, her obsessive nature and dedication to getting every detail right made her excel in the role. When the store owner drowned two years earlier, with no known relatives, the young half-elf had inherited the small apothecary. Such luck was unheard of among the half-elves of Sandcastle.

'What do you want?' asked Rayn.

Ada hadn't seen Rayn in months and needed a few breaths to adjust her expectations to her former roommate's confrontational style of dialogue.

'Nice to see you, too,' Ada answered, trying to keep the exchange civil.

'Your boyfriend left you for someone else?' Rayn prodded. 'No!' Ada said, instinctively, before she admitted defeat. 'I left him after he slept with someone else. How did you know?'

'You only come when your boys beat you or sleep with someone else. Or both.'

'That's not true!'

'Yes, it is. What do you want from me?'

Ada took some time to recall her visits to Rayn over the last couple of years and realised that Rayn's statement was not entirely inaccurate. She discarded half a dozen denials, before settling on the only way that worked with Rayn.

'You are right. I need a place to sleep for a few nights. Until I can find something else. Please?'

'You can sleep under the counter. Don't steal from the shelves,' Rayn replied and turned her back to her, seemingly disinterested in further conversation on the subject.

Ada drew her breath sharply and was about to deny the accusations of theft. Again, Rayn spoke the truth. Indeed, on several occasions, Ada had pilfered exotic herbs from the store, desiring to experiment with their recreational effects.

'I'm sorry,' she said, meekly.

'You are, now,' Rayn said.

Chapter 4: Sewer

Gilmir spewed out the foul water and drew in a ragged breath. He remembered falling and landing in water. No, not water, but the barely liquid sludge of the sewer.

'This is the second time I save your life within a quartermark, Stick Elf,' the halfling said.

The short saviour stood over him with a less-than-impressed expression on his face. Gilmir's body convulsed again, trying to eject more of the sewage. It was remarkable how much strength his weakened body mustered from the reflex, far beyond his voluntary command. He considered answering the annoying creature looking down at him, but had no retort. His back lay against the rough stones of a narrow ledge running by the sewer canal. Above, the trapdoor through which they had descended was closed. The air was cool and damp. The stench of human waste filled his nostrils.

'We need to move,' the halfling said, looking up. 'The guards will come searching any moment now.'

Gilmir stretched out his arm. Noting that the halfling had said 'we'. He studied the little fellow. His hands were slender with nimble fingers. His body appeared strong, lean and lacking the round belly so typical for the food-loving people. Despite his young face, he had a confident demeanour. Indicative of experience beyond his years. Based on the way he had opened the cell door, he was probably a thief. By choice or necessity, Gilmir knew not. And that meant he did not know why the halfling had helped him, either. Another worry. He could, however, see that the thief had not been in prison for very long. The halfling took Gilmir's hand and dragged him to his feet with ease.

'What's your name?' Gilmir asked, studying the short figure in front of him with new interest.

'Fox,' said the halfling.

Gilmir raised his eyebrows.

Fox shrugged, turned and stalked down the passage. Gilmir coughed, spat and went after him, steadying himself with one hand on the moist wall. In the sparse light, the halfling moved slow, allowing Gilmir to keep up.

Two hundred careful steps later, the tunnel came to a stop. The sewer seemed to continue straight down. There was no apparent way out. Fox stood on the ledge, looking down where the foul water fell away.

'I guess we have to follow the sewer,' the thief said and threw a glance at Gilmir as he caught up.

Gilmir sat down and put his back against the slimy, fungus-covered wall. After a moment staring down the plunging sewer, he said, 'Drowning in human waste is quickly rising to the top of my list of *the worst ways to die*.'

He shook his head and lifted his gaze to the halfling. 'Listen, I cannot come up with a single reason why you should come back to warn me if you discern that the swim is more likely to kill me than get me out of here. But, if you would ... I cannot express how much I would rather just die here on this ledge. Of starvation. Or the stench ...'

Some emotion flickered in Fox's eyes. Compassion? Pity? Gilmir could not bear it.

'But, hey! Come to think of it, a halfling saving an elf three times in a quarter of an hour has to be some kind of record!' Gilmir tried to smile. It felt like a grimace.

Fox glanced from Gilmir to the sewer and back again. 'I suspect these tunnels will be the death of you and me both.'

Without another word, he pinched his nose and jumped feet first into the water.

Gilmir closed his eyes and rested his head on the wall. He hoped the halfling made it out. Dying in the dungeon of this corrupted city was something he would not wish for his worst enemy. Whatever the little halfling was, he certainly was not that. A draft prickled against Gilmir's neck. He shivered. He was wet and cold. His mind formed dark thoughts, and his mood kept spiralling downward.

A splash sounded, and Gilmir forced his eyelids open. Fox came to the surface. He shook his wet hair from his eyes and spat. Locking gaze with Gilmir, he said, 'It's too far. You would not make it, elf. I'm sorry.'

Then, he was gone once more, leaving Gilmir alone.

To die.

Chapter 5: Fire

Crack!

Ada awoke, disoriented and afraid. Forcing herself to lie still, she browsed her recent memories for clues about time and place: Zac's betrayal, muddy streets, Rayn, the apothecary.

The floor creaked under heavy feet by the door. Not daring to move, Ada reached out beyond the limits of her own consciousness. There was a presence in the room, with an overwhelmingly strong will. A purpose. She felt it searching, intensely, scanning the room like the beam from a lighthouse.

'Light,' she thought.

The room was dark, except the sparse moonlight finding its way through two dirty windows. The intruder didn't bring any light sources. Didn't need any. The floorboards groaned as he moved towards the wall within touching distance from the counter under which Ada was concealed. Ada clenched her fists to her chest to keep her hands from trembling as she heard him shuffling the vials and cups on the shelves. A sudden wave of satisfaction emanated from the presence. No, not satisfaction, she realised. There was no element of joy, only fulfilment. Completion.

Ada shivered as the intruder walked past her hiding place on his way to the narrow stairs leading up to Rayn's chambers on the loft. He smelled of wet wool and decay. The old, wooden stairs complained loudly and threatened to break for each step.

'I must alert Rayn,' Ada thought, and dared to peek over the counter.

The silhouette confirmed her previous assumptions: a tall man in his thirties, the muscular upper body bared. His head moved slowly from his right to his left, apparently scanning the room. Whether he was using his eyes or relied on some other sense, Ada could not say.

He stopped momentarily as his gaze found Ada, motionless on her knees behind the counter less than six feet away. For several moments they appraised each other until he discarded Ada as non-essential to his mission and continued his ascent.

Ada grabbed the sack with her belongings and ran for the door.

A wordless scream inside her head made her stop before she reached the relative safety of the dark alleys outside. She turned, reluctantly, in time to see the intruder disappear through the trapdoor in the ceiling.

'I don't want to die!' screamed the voice in her head.

'Get out!' Ada yelled. She dropped her sack, drew her pocketknife and ran up the stairs.

The loft was warm. Flickering light emanated from the vents in the oven, illuminating the scene. Rayn, in her nightgown, tried to keep a table between the large man and herself. Arms outstretched, he ignored the table altogether and walked straight at her, driving his prey into a corner. As the low roof forced him to bend awkwardly, Ada seized the opportunity to rush forward and thrust her knife deep into the side of his neck.

Nothing happened.

Ignoring the knife, the man seized the table blocking his path to the frightened half-elf, and tossed it aside.

Spurred by desperation and the assailant's lack of interest in her, Ada grabbed the only chair in the loft and smashed it over his head. He made no sound, but turned his head towards her. Just in time for her to stab the broken chair leg into his face, lacerating the skin on his left cheek. Still, he neither bled nor uttered a single word. This time, however, he acknowledged Ada's presence as an unwanted disturbance.

Turning his back to Rayn, he backhanded Ada with such force that she partly flew, partly slid on the floor to the other side of the room. Before she got back on her feet, he was after her. She retreated further until her back was touching the hot metal of the oven. The courage she possessed moments before disappeared as soon as he turned his unblinking eyes on her. Futilely, she grabbed his arms, as cold fingers tightened around her neck. Through her tears, she saw the torn flesh in his face.

This man did not bleed. Did not blink. Did not breathe.

As his fingers strangled her, the oven singed the skin on her back. Ada could not move. In desperation, she closed her eyes and channelled the heat away from the exposed area. The essence of fire flowed through her veins like warm liquid. Her mind fell quiet. The grip around her neck relaxed a little, allowing her to inhale.

She opened her eyes to witness flames erupting from her hands, engulfing the arms of the man attempting to choke her. The smell of burnt hair and flesh was intense, but she did not flinch. Soon, the scorched muscles and tendons in his lower arms and hands weakened the grip around her neck, and Ada managed to wriggle loose.

A loud crack emanated as Rayn rammed the table into the man, unbalancing him. The half-elf grabbed Ada by the shoulder and pulled her away.

'Run!' Rayn said.

Gasping for breath, Ada scrambled towards the trapdoor and followed Rayn down the stairs. She picked up her sack while Rayn hastily picked some items from a shelf. The intruder half ran, half fell down the stairs, as they burst out the door.

Chapter 6: Door

Someone was talking. As for who, when and where, Gilmir could not say. He was not awake. Nor dead. Too much pain for that. Something inside urged him to wake up. His old instincts refused to let go. Refused to let him die. The voices came again. Muffled. As if they originated from behind a wall. Or, a heavy door. *A door?* There was not supposed to be a door here. He forced his eyes open. In the dark, a weak, green light radiated from the walls of a tunnel. The sewer. The prison. Someone spoke behind him. The wall at his back trembled. He closed his eyes again. *Why should he care?* His heart thumped. Hard. Once more, his body tried telling him something. In an extraordinary exertion of force, he shuffled into the corner of the corridor. Away from the moving wall.

The door swung out, hiding the person opening it from sight. Light flooded into the tunnel. Gilmir squinted. When the door closed, he would be in full view. He shut his eyes, willing the shadows to engulf him. A hollow thump sounded. Flickering torchlight.

'Hey, what's this?' a gruff voice asked.

Gilmir quickly considered his options. There were none. He was utterly at the mercy of the two human brutes. How far he had fallen. He opened his mouth to speak but shut it as soon as his eyes fell upon the two men.

'What do you mean?' replied the other man. A short, bald fellow. The torchlight reflected from his smooth pate. *Candle*, Gilmir decided to name him, following the thoughtless human tradition of this rat-infested corner of the world. That is, the custom to name something after its defining trait. The city above, for instance, was called Shacktown. The mountain range to the east with the jagged peaks was called Jaw Mountains. It made you wonder how many rivers were called *Waterflow*?

His instincts told him to focus. He shifted his gaze to the other man. The one dressed and built like a street thug. Dirt made his tanned skin darker. Crooked teeth behind thin lips made Gilmir think about a shark. *Shark*, then.

'Look at the wall, Dick,' Shark said, gesturing with his free hand. 'The fungus.'

Dick? Perfect. Gilmir thought, too tired to smile.

'What about it?' Dick said.

'It's dead. The fungus covering the door is dark. Almost black. Dead.'

'So what?'

'It's just strange,' Shark said. 'Look at the shape, it's almost—'

'I don't care about the fungus, let's finish this.'

Shark shrugged. The two men started down the corridor, leaving mud stains on the floor.

'So, how are we to come by fifty silver?' Dick asked.

'We'll borrow it. From Voan.'

'Voan?' Dick stopped and turned to Shark. 'Do you really mean to loan the money from Voan, to buy the stone, and sell it to Voan?'

'Yes. And then pay him back. Brilliant, eh?'

'I don't know … will he even loan you that much?'

'He is desperate for such a stone. That's well known. Besides, he knows we won't get far in a day. He will take the risk. No one is stupid enough to cheat Voan.'

The men continued down the corridor.

'I'm not sure. Something tells me this is a bad idea.'

'Relax, Dick. At this time tomorrow it will all be over.'

Gilmir stared after the men. He ought to follow.

Time passed, and he did not move. Closing his eyes, he thought about what the men had said. His head hurt. Apparently, they had made contact with someone willing to sell a stone. A valuable stone that Voan wanted. They probably came directly from the meeting. On their way to speak to Voan? Did they work for him? Perhaps in some capacity. Tomorrow they would meet this stone seller again and, hopefully, they would take the same path.

If the stone was what Gilmir thought, he needed it.

And a thief. He also needed a thief.

Chapter 7: Sandcastle

'This way,' Ada said, and grabbed Rayn's hand.

Ada knew the streets of Sandcastle well, by night and by day. The two girls ran through dark alleys, climbed walls and fences, and jumped from roof to roof until they reached the gate at the outer city wall. Their pursuer was nowhere to be seen, and they allowed themselves to slow their pace before they approached the guards in front of the gate.

Sandcastle was so named because of its striking similarity to castles children would build on beaches in the summer. Located on a natural island some two hundred yards off the western coast, the city was magnificent to behold with its tall, white spires behind several concentric circles of yellow stone walls. At low tide, a person might walk or ride on the wet sand between the city and the mainland. Carts and wagons—as well as siege engines in wartime—would inevitably get stuck until the waves washed them away hours later. When the tide was high, goods and people would be brought to and from the city on flat bottomed boats, most of them owned by the mayor himself.

'How's the tide?' Ada asked before the guards could initiate their bothersome routine questions. Nobody left the city through the main gates in the middle of the night without a compelling explanation.

'Eh, it was low an hour ago. Why?' one of the guards replied.

'Perfect, we can make it over if we're quick,' Ada said, and walked past the guards, towards the gate. 'If we don't make it across before dawn, I will be dead,' she added.

The guards hesitated and glanced to each other for guidance.

'You can't leave the city tonight. You have to wait until morning, and hire a barge,' said the eldest of the two guards.

'We'd love to,' Ada said. 'But then I will be dead.'

She turned her back to them and showed the burned skin under singed clothes.

The guards grimaced as they briefly examined her wounds from a safe distance. 'Very well, you may pass,' the guard said at last. He handed Ada his torch. 'Take this. It will last until you're ashore.'

'Thank you, and bless your noble and benevolent souls,' Ada said, curtsying for good measure. They slipped out the gates as soon as the guards opened them.

'Why did we have to leave the city?' Rayn asked, as the pair took their first steps into the ankle-deep water separating Sandcastle from the mainland.

'I felt his presence and intentions as soon as he entered the store. He was no common burglar. He was searching for *you*,' Ada said.

'No, he wasn't.'

'Why do you say that? He came straight at you and ignored everything else. He didn't even notice me, until I poked his eye out.'

'No. He came for this,' Rayn replied, and pulled out a black pendant attached to a chain around her neck. Its polished sides shone in the torchlight. 'Besides, the reason the man ignored you is that he was already dead.'

'What? How do you know?'

'What of it? The pendant, or the dead man?' Rayn frowned. She never had much tolerance for ambiguity.

'Well, both!' Ada said. The water was knee-deep now, and they were not even halfway across.

'My shard pendant has a twin. I kept it on the shelf in the store. I went to pick it up before we fled, but the man had stolen it before he climbed the stairs to the loft.'

'Yes, he did take something from the shelves. But how do you know he was dead?'

'Because he didn't breathe, bleed or feel any pain.'

'That's ridiculous!' Ada threw a quick glance towards the city, half expecting to be chased through the water by a dead man.

'Maybe.'

Ada stopped and looked down at the waves washing against her thighs. 'It's cold, and my back hurts like a hundred floggings. Why don't you just toss the pendant in the sea, and we can go back to the store?'

'I can't.'

'Why not?'

'Because the shard is part of me. We're bonded,' Rayn said.

'What does that mean?'

'I just told you. It's a part of me. If I lose she shard, I lose part of myself.'

'Like a pet dog?'

'No. Not like a dog. Like a soul-bound shard,' Rayn said, shivering. 'Do you want to stay here much longer?'

'I'm sorry.' Ada resumed walking towards the shore.

They waded through the water in silence until the first waves reached the exposed burns on Ada's back. She yelped in pain but kept walking.

Chapter 8: Saendar

Gilmir woke. Again. This time he did not think he had slept for long. For some reason, he felt better. Perhaps a purpose, an objective, was what he had needed. Something obtainable in the near future. Rising, he turned towards the wall. Shark had been right; the fungus on the wall was dead. Gilmir chose to ignore the matter and focused on the hidden door. His fingers searched for the edges. It did not take long—the door was a crude one. After finding the outline, it took a few beats to find the bump serving as a handle. He slid the handle, and the door started to tremble and move. A narrow passage opened up. Gilmir stepped inside and closed the door behind him. It was dark, completely dark, and the going was slow. One thousand five hundred and twenty-five steps later, he came to a door outlined by daylight seeping through the cracks. He pushed it open and stepped out.

Closing his eyes, he turned towards the sun. *Falling stars!* It was nice to feel the sun on his face. He was out. He was out! For the first time in two and a half years, he was free. Had he not been so weak, he would have danced. Something he had not done since his youth back home in Darieth. Before he started his service. Back when his life had some element of fun and joy. Or innocence. His new life would be more like that. Simple, joyful. Free. If he could just survive these first days. Regain his strength. Some semblance of his strength, at least. Now, he was frail as a kitten. An easy target. Prey. He opened his eyes.

Great trees surrounded him. He was standing in a small grove, and sunlight filtered through branches and leaves. Birds sang, leaves rustled, and to his right ran a stream. His mouth was dry as autumn leaves and still tasted like human waste. He walked towards the water. After an arduous walk of a hundred feet, he fell to his knees by the bank, submerged his face and drank.

Afterwards, he bathed and washed his ragged clothes. His long hair was a mess, with lumps that had to be cut out as soon as he found something sharp. His black silken shirt was in tatters. The soft leather vest frayed, and his linen trousers had more holes in them than an orcish battle plan. His shoes were long gone, the same with his leather greaves. However, better than nothing and now cleaner than they had been for ages, he put the clothes back on.

Gilmir started down a path heading in the direction of the city. Soon the path joined with a larger one, and within a mark, he stepped out on one of the main roads. Already exhausted, he was on the verge of giving up before he got to the outskirts. The part that had given the city its name. Hundreds of rickety buildings clung to each other like drunken human teenagers. He heard horses approaching but could not spare the energy to turn. After a few more beats, someone shouted.

'Move! Out of the way!'

Gilmir lifted his gaze, trying to find who was blocking the path of the riders.

'Hey you, beggar, move! Are you deaf or something!'

Realising that the human rider was talking to him, Gilmir bit back a retort and stepped to the side. The two riders did not spare him another glance. They were clearing the path for a caravan of some sort. Behind them came four heavily armoured guards riding two and two. Following them were large, decorated wagons. A bored-looking crossbowman sat beside the driver. From inside the cart, Gilmir heard cheering, the clinks of glasses, and laughter. This was one of Voan's caravans, bringing in nobles from other cities to watch the games. Rich people paying good money to watch less fortunate people being hurt or killed. An explicit picture of human nature, if there ever was one.

Dark thoughts on the subject of human nature accompanied Gilmir as he closed the distance to the city. He set his target on getting past the new parts of the town and getting into the city proper. As soon as he passed under the old city gate, he slumped to the ground. Halfway crawling, he moved to put his back against the wall. If he could just live to execute the plan. If he could stay alive for another day, he would make it. For the next couple of hours, he spent his time asking people passing by if they knew a halfling called Fox. Few bothered to answer, and no one recognised the description.

He wondered if he had the strength to get up and move to another location, when he noticed a small, bald man walking towards him with the practised steps of a veteran drunk. The man had only a stump for a right arm and held a bottle in his left hand. He slid to the ground beside Gilmir and passed him the bottle.

'Wine? You look thirsty.'

Gilmir took the bottle and drank. The wine was warm and sour. He had to stop himself from drinking it all. The old man was probably stingy about his wine. Gilmir handed the bottle back.

'Thank you.'

'You're welcome. I'm Saendar, who are you?'

Gilmir turned and studied the man. Saendar pulled the cork out of the bottle with his teeth and spat it on the ground. Then he drank. He looked the part of the town drunkard.

'I am Darieth,' said Gilmir.

The old man nodded but said nothing. He held the bottle out for Gilmir once more. Gilmir took it and drank. Less this time. After passing the bottle back, he asked, "Have you heard of a halfling called Fox?'

'Fox?' Saendar took another swig. 'No, there is no halfling with that name here.'

'How do you know?'

Saendar shrugged.

Gilmir was spent, hungry, in pain and really annoyed with the fact that he seemed destined to die the same day he escaped the dungeons. With the prospect of getting the tool so close, he needed to get his life back together. That nobody could help him with the easy task of finding a halfling in a human town intensified his annoyance. His desperation.

'Why would a human drunkard know anything worth knowing?' Gilmir turned away. He would have liked to stand up and leave, but he did not have the energy.

'Don't be so quick to dismiss people you don't know. One day you will stumble upon your equal, and not even recognise it.'

'One day, perhaps, but this day all I see is the town drunkard.'

'Really? Is that *all*?'

'Of course not. I see an old man, who has lost his self-worth years ago, along with his sword arm. In all likelihood an ex-soldier. Now he walks around feeling sorry for himself, and when the sorrow gets too pronounced, he tries to bury it with drink. Every day at about mid-morning, that is. And, when his spirit lifts a shade, and he wants more, he seeks out people who are even worse off, so he can feel better about himself. Sharing, though he has little to share, makes him more generous than the most benevolent king. Drinking in every tavern in town, he knows a lot of people, and more know him. Or they know *of* him. Because no one knows the things that matter. Which means they actually do not care. Nevertheless, he thinks this knowledge makes him so important, and he talks about the town like he owns it. Trying every mark of every hour to find some way to convince himself that he still has some value as a human, even though he is as worthless as a soldier without his sword arm. *That* is the sorry creature I see before me, old man.'

Saendar rose and looked like he was going to walk away without saying another word. Then he turned.

'You are right,' he nodded like in deep thought, 'although I am disappointed in the lack of sophistication in your description. A town drunkard could do better.'

Gilmir scoffed.

'I would have thought a high-born elf would be better trained,' Saendar said and turned his back towards Gilmir.

Gilmir shook his head, ready to dismiss the man and all he had said when an alarm in his head started ringing. Loud and intense. Why had the man marked him as a high-born? That was strange. That was … dangerous.

'What do you mean?' Gilmir said before Saendar had taken more than a few steps. The old man turned again. His eyes hinted at a smile that did not reach his lips.

'I mean,' said Saendar, 'that I am disappointed. You are clearly not in your best shape, but I expected more. You look like a beggar. Ragged clothes, thin and sickly. You have recently taken a bath and washed your clothes. Your pale skin reveals you haven't seen the sun for months. You have had much to eat. Where have you been? My guess, in prison. You couldn't have gone far in your condition. The dungeons here in town? Few are kept there for long. Years? Why? Did they think someone would pay for your ransom? Which means you are important. And you wrinkled your nose after tasting my wine. The first decent thing you've had to drink in months? Years? Used to drinking wine of different quality altogether, I would guess. But why did nobody pay your ransom? Because they didn't want to acknowledge you. You were not worth it. Not even to your family? So, a third son, a fourth? A bastard? Trained to be a spy? An assassin? On a mission that went wrong.' The old man studied Gilmir before he continued.

'And you gave me a false name. Elves are seldom named after places in my experience, and last time I checked, Darieth was a small elven city. You lied out of habit but did a sloppy job of it. Perhaps you didn't think it necessary. Maybe you are exhausted, in pain and close to giving up. Your clothes are of quality, although only rags now, you used to carry two swords—one short and one long—and you are still alive. Which all fits the bill of a highly trained elven agent of some sort. Fallen far, but still. However, your sloppy analysis, your careless lying, your ignorant neglect of a potential ally when you are in dire need of one, suggest something else entirely. So perhaps I am wrong.' Saendar shrugged.

Gilmir stared at the man. Speechless.

'There is a halfling down by the Bits Arena, which could've been the one giving you the name 'Fox'. Good luck getting your life back together, and count your blessings that you didn't offend this old drunkard.'

Saendar walked off with measured steps. Leaving the almost empty wine bottle at Gilmir's side.

Chapter 9: Bargetown

Bargetown consisted of three large storehouses, a guardhouse, an inn and a stable. The town's sole purpose was to maintain the supply chain to Sandcastle. The activity at the two piers was not regulated by night and day but by the ebbing or rising tide. At high tide, the barges would make as many passes back and forth as possible. When the water was low, their crew would rest until the next burst. Goods arriving at low tide would be unloaded in the storehouses next to the pier, and the merchants, drivers and guards would pass the hours at the inn.

As the two young women climbed the stairs to the pier, the first of the townspeople and travellers were already preparing to start loading the barges. None of them seemed to take an interest in the new arrivals.

'Can you see him?' Ada asked, looking back at the sea that now separated them from the city of Sandcastle.

'No. It's d-dark. I c-can't see anything out t-there,' Rayn replied through chattering teeth.

'I thought elves had night vision.'

'They d-do. I'm a half-elf. I've got my father's eyes.'

'Did you know your father?' Ada asked. She had never heard Rayn mention him before.

'No. He ran away with his war band after he'd raped my mother,' Rayn replied. Only the sudden absence of the chattering of teeth revealed her altered emotional state.

'I'm sorry.'

'Yes.'

Ada endured the awkward silence, which was made more agonising by the increasing pain from her wounds as the numbing effects of the water faded. She thought of jumping off the pier again, but the vivid memories of the first exposure to the saltwater made her consider her options.

'There is a fire in the city. Look!' The relief was so evident in her voice, she sounded almost joyful.

Rayn turned towards the city and the red light flickering in the distance. There was neither relief nor joy in her voice as she said, 'That's my shop burning.'

'No! That can't be! Who would set fire to your shop?'

Rayn turned to face her, tears welling up in her eyes. 'You did.'

Ada opened her mouth to deny the accusation, but could not find the words. She remembered the flames spouting from her hands, scorching the intruder's arms. But the experience was so unlike her, so alien, that she could not comprehend that she had done it. Or rather, it had been her, but a different kind of her. Some version of her she had never known.

'I'm sorry,' Ada whispered.

'Yes.' Rayn wiped the tears from her face.

Ada put her arm around her friend. 'You're cold. Come, let's find some shelter and some dry clothes.'

Soon, they were huddling under blankets on a bench in front of the inn's fireplace. Ada had no difficulties persuading the innkeeper's wife to let them sit by the fire until dawn. She even reheated the leftovers from last night's stew, which they quickly devoured.

'I can help you with your wounds,' Rayn said without preamble.

'Really? How?' Ada asked, not accustomed to Rayn knowing anything remotely useful.

'I make healing salves from stone. I grabbed two vials from the shop before we fled.'

'From the shard?'

'No. But the shard helps me prepare it better.'

'What are those shards anyway?' Ada said.

'Shards from the starfall.'

'Which starfall?'

'The starfall twenty years ago. You don't remember?'

'I wasn't born twenty years ago. I'm nineteen,' Ada said.

'I remember the starfall. I lived in the forest not far from here with my mother. Before she died.'

'I'm sorry.'

'Yes.' Rayn rose, carefully removed the blanket from Ada's shoulders and produced a yellow vial from some unseen pocket in her nightgown. 'Lay on the bench, face down.'

Ada did as she was told, and Rayn removed the burnt edges of her shirt, fully exposing her wounds.

'You've been lucky,' the half-elf said. 'The oven burned a hole in your shirt, but most of the skin underneath only has moderate damage. Maybe the cold water helped reduce the severity of the injuries?'

'Perhaps.' Ada did not accept the explanation. Her skin had been burnt as she was pushed up against the oven. But it stopped when she started channelling the heat through her body. Despite never experiencing anything like that before, it had been so easy. She knew exactly what to do at that moment. Because she had to do it just like that.

'Lie still.' Rayn started applying something on Ada's naked back.

'That doesn't feel like a salve,' Ada remarked.

Rayn sprinkled a pinch of white sand in Ada's open hand. 'It will, soon, when the stone interacts with your blood.'

Rayn put away the yellow vial and lay her hands gently on Ada's back. The pain subsided.

'What's happening?' Ada said.

Rayn spoke slowly as she moved her hands a few inches, back and forth. 'The sand absorbs the blood and moisture from the wound, and transforms.' She reached out with her hand for Ada to examine the brown salve smeared in her palm. 'It's a healing salve, especially effective against burns.'

'It feels cool,' Ada mumbled and dozed off.

Chapter 10: Flight

'It's here,' the voice inside her head said.

Ada stirred and opened her eyes. 'We must go,' she said.

She untangled herself from Rayn, who had fallen asleep on top of her on the bench. Draping the blanket over her shoulders, she covered her naked back.

'Get up, Rayn, we must run!'

As Rayn got to her feet, a man screamed outside the inn. Moments later, the door was flung open, and a soaking wet man entered. His clothing was torn, and his pale skin shone through in several places. Despite his dishevelled state, there was no doubt it was the same man who had attacked them in Rayn's shop the night before. A deep cut bared the bone right below his left shoulder and caused the arm to swing unnaturally along the side of his body. The most notable difference, however, was the sword that was stuck in his chest. It protruded a foot or so out of his back.

They ran. Through the kitchen and out the back door, past the stables and over the grazing fields.

'Where?' Rayn asked.

Ada turned her head while she ran and found the dead man chasing them, some fifty yards behind. 'Head for the trees!'

Ada had made her mind up in a beat. She based her decision on the assumption that the dead man's sheer size would be a disadvantage when running through a forest. Soon, she questioned her wisdom, as several options came to mind. They were running away from other people, away from anyone who could have helped them. Instead, they should have entered a barge at the pier, or even dived into the sea. Surely, the guards would be able to keep their pursuer occupied for long enough for them to slip away.

Or would they?

She remembered the sword lodged in the dead man's torso. Of course, the guards had tried to stop him, only to learn that their killing blows hardly slowed their opponent at all.

How do you kill something already dead? How do you fight it? How do you outrun it?

Again, Ada turned to look behind. The dead man had not gained on them.

'We run faster than him!' she said, a hint of hope in her voice.

'Yes,' Rayn replied, short of breath, 'but for how long?'

Any hope Ada harboured, left her. They could run a mile, perhaps two, at this pace. Maybe more in favourable terrain. But sooner or later they would tire, and their unyielding hunter would catch them. Fuelled by desperation, they reached the woods.

Ada's assumptions proved to be right. Between the trees, the two slender women moved faster than the sluggish brute chasing them. But there was a price: Before long, they were bleeding from dozens of cuts from the branches and bushes that had whipped them as they fled. Dodging branches, changing direction and jumping over roots and streams drained their stamina fast. Caution and exhaustion eventually forced them to slow the pace and soon after they heard heavy steps behind them, gaining on them.

Seeing a clearing to the right, they seized the opportunity and left the forest. Their flight had taken them far from Sandcastle and Bargetown by the coast, and the Jaw Mountains loomed in the east, another two or three leagues away. Far beyond their reach.

Their initial relief of being able to run in a straight line without worrying about when a branch would take an eye, was short-lived. They soon learned that the soft ground and tall grass favoured the man chasing them. Every step more laborious, like running through water, they could no longer keep their distance to the dead man.

'Drop the stone!' Ada yelled to her friend in front of her.

'No!' Rayn cried.

Ada didn't dare to look behind. She knew that each heavy step brought him closer, and she almost felt his cold fingers around her neck. In desperation, she veered to the left, choosing a different route than her friend. As she expected, the dead man followed Rayn, followed the stone.

Ada was soon back on his trail, hunting the hunter. Somehow, the sword was still stuck, and the tip that protruded from his back bobbed up and down as he ran. Spending her last breaths of air, she closed the distance between her and the dead man and threw herself at his ankles. His feet momentarily entwined, he fell flat on the ground. The impact pushed the sword up to the hilt. Foul-smelling pus squirted out from his back as another foot of blade was forced out of his back.

'No!' Ada shouted as the dead man got to his feet in front of her. He paid no attention to her but examined the sword hilt as if he just then noticed that he was carrying the extra burden. Clutching both hands around the pommel, he pulled. Slowly, the sword wedged between his ribs loosened, and he drew it out and tossed it to the ground before resuming his chase.

'No!' Ada screamed again, lying helpless in the tall grass as the dead man hunted down Rayn. She closed her eyes and reached out, searching for the half-elf's spirit. Ignoring the mindless chattering of nearby creatures, she found Rayn, unguarded and afraid, facing the predator's cold presence. The noise coalesced into a high-pitched shriek, as Ada trespassed on her friend's mind, forcing her own will through the barrier that separated them.

'*Drop the stone!*' Ada commanded, without uttering a single word.

Rayn yelped like a kicked dog, and tossed her shard pendant to the ground

Chapter 11: Purpose

'You were in my head!' Rayn screamed as Ada approached her.

Despite gasping for air, the half-elf was still standing, tears reflecting the evening sun as she faced Ada.

'I'm sorry,' Ada said. 'I had to, or you would be dead by now.'

'The shard is part of me!'

'The rest of you still lives.' Ada reached for her friend's naked shoulder, bleeding from many small cuts. 'Let's go home.'

Rayn pulled away from her. 'I don't have a home any more.'

The events of the night before flashed through Ada's mind. Zac had broken her heart, but that meant nothing now. Her heart was still beating. The fire, the flight. The magic. Something had changed. Everything had changed. For both of them.

'You can't know your shop burned. It could be any other building,' Ada said, half-heartedly. Of course, it was the apothecary that burned.

'Yes, I can. For certain.'

'How?'

'Because I felt it as we ran through the city. I sensed their distress.'

'What? Whose distress?'

'The stones. The crystals in my shop,' Rayn gazed towards the mountains in the east.

'Are you still talking to stones?' Ada laughed.

Rayn couldn't help herself from smiling. 'I never stopped. I learned not to let anybody notice.'

Relieved to have managed to calm her friend, Ada bent and picked up a stone from the ground. 'Can you talk to this?'

'I could,' Rayn replied. The half-elf pulled up a blade of grass and offered it to Ada. 'Eat this, and tell me how it feels.'

Hesitantly, Ada accepted the grass and chewed. 'Doesn't taste much.'

Rayn kept quiet.

'What's your point?' Ada asked, eventually.

'Why don't you eat more?'

'Because grass doesn't nourish me. Eating grass serves no purpose.'

'Exactly, and that's why I don't talk to the stone in your hand. It serves no purpose.'

'But some stones are worth talking to?' Ada was only beginning to comprehend.

'Yes. All stones are not equal. Neither are all plants or animals. A dog is more than a rat. A rat is more than a worm. You would not talk to a worm, because it serves no purpose.'

Ada nodded, remembering the noise from the incomprehensible thoughts and emotions from nearby birds and rodents as she'd reached out from Rayn's spirit. 'The worm has nothing to say.'

'Neither does your stone, nor the grass beneath our feet.'

'But your pendant does?'

Again, Rayn turned her head and gazed in the direction of the Jaw Mountains. 'Yes, the shard speaks to me even now. But its voice is faint, weaker for every mile between us.'

Ada briefly examined the cuts and bruises on her arms and feet. Thanks to the healing salve Rayn applied that morning, the burns on her back did not hurt.

She glanced at Rayn. Blood covered more of her skin than her torn nightgown did. So fragile. So vulnerable.

Ada shook her head at their predicament. She briefly considered going back for the sword the dead man dropped but discarded the idea. Neither of them was proficient with a sword, and drawing attention by trying to sell a sword that so obviously did not belong to them would only get them into more trouble. 'Alright, let's find your stone.'

'Shard,' Rayn said.

Chapter 12: Fox

Gilmir was worried. Not about dying. He had been dying for months, and had grown accustomed to the ongoing experience. What worried him was how the bald little man seemed to know so much about him. Of course, not everything was true. Then he would have been sure. Sure, the old man recognised him from somewhere, at some time. They had met before. Did he discern all that from his observations? His reasoning was sound. The logic was valid.

However, how could he have discerned that Gilmir used to carry two swords? He glanced down to his ragged trousers. Examined the fabric in his hands. Was the linen more worn out where the swords had been hanging? Had the dangling scabbards rubbed the cloth at specific points?

At his now-lost greaves, sure, but he did not see much of a mark on the trousers. He lifted his hands to study them. Swordsmen often had larger muscles between the thumb and index finger. Nevertheless, the same could be said about everyone using heavy tools. Both of Gilmir's hands showed traces of these telltale muscles, but like every other muscle in his body, they had shrunk to shadows of what was.

If Saendar deduced who he was, Gilmir was in danger. Could his life be in any more peril? Probably not, but death was hardly the worst of fates. Going back to that hellhole, for instance. It did not matter at this point. He had enough on his plate. Somehow, he had to live through the next day. He had to get to the meeting place and steal the stone. Moreover, if he was to have any hope of doing any of these things, he needed help. He had no one to trust, but at least he knew of someone who had helped him before. The halfling was still the logical choice. He did not know how to find him, however. Gilmir shook his head and emptied the bottle of wine. This Saendar was right about the sour wine.

Gilmir lay his head back against the wall and closed his eyes.

Thump. Something hit his foot. *Thump.* Again. In his dream, he kept bumping his foot into the next step of the stairs up the Blessed Tower. He tried lifting it extra high for the next step. *Thump.* It did not help.

'You finally dead?'

Gilmir opened his eyes. Fox stood in front of him, kicking at his foot. At least he looked like Fox. Something was different, though. The small figure stood leaning on a staff. The left foot was bent at the ankle, looking deformed.

'What happened to your foot?'

'It has always been like this. Have you lost your mind also?' The halfling glanced around before he changed the topic. 'I heard rumours that some elf beggar was asking around for Fox the halfling. What do you want?'

'Believe it or not, I need your help,' Gilmir said, and got up to a sitting position. He must have fallen over while sleeping. Brushing at his arm, he tried to remove some mud from his shirt.

'Yeah, that's hard to believe! I remember setting some kind of record for saving the life of an elf the most times in less than an hour.'

'You are a remarkable halfling.'

'Your praise is heart-warming,' Fox said without enthusiasm while he put both hands to his chest.

'Listen,' said Gilmir, 'I really need your help once again. I will make it worth your while. I am not sure how at this time, but I'll find a way.'

Fox stared down at him for a long while. Gilmir did not know what more he should say.

'For some reason, I believe you,' Fox responded at last. 'I've never seen someone as weak as you were in the sewer, survive. You don't seem to be completely out of the woods yet, but why shouldn't I save your life for the fourth time? At some point you'll have to start paying me back, one would think.'

'Out of the woods? You sound like one of these stupid shack-dwellers.'

'Okay, you insolent tree-hugger of a stick elf, the first rule if you want someone to help you: do not insult them!'

'The *first* rule?'

'Yeah, I'm sure there will be more coming before this—whatever it is—is over.'

Gilmir sighed. 'I am sorry. You did not deserve that. I am so damned tired of being helpless. I'll try hard to abide by the rule.'

'*Rules.*'

'Sure, rules.'

'There you go!' Fox held out his hand. 'I think the first thing we need to do is to get you some food. And afterwards, you can tell me how I can help you.'

Gilmir took the outstretched hand. The halfling was surprisingly strong and dragged him to his feet. 'How did you know I needed help for something more than food?'

'Just a feeling. By the way, I go by the name Hobble around here,' the halfling previously known as Fox said, and started limping down the street.

'I can see why,' Gilmir said, 'I am called Gilmir most places.' He did not bother with another lie.

Chapter 13: Power

'What makes your stones so special?' Ada asked.

The two women had stopped to drink from a stream, and took the opportunity to wash away some blood and dirt from their faces and hands. They had been alternating between jogging and brisk walking for an hour, always following Rayn's pendant towards the Jaw Mountains.

'Shards,' Rayn mumbled, before she raised her voice to a normal level. 'It all depends on how they are created. The more power that goes into making a stone, or an item, or a being, the more powerful it will be. The shards are fragments of a star, and the stars were made by the sun on The First Day. Part of the sun's power is embedded in every shard.'

'Power?'

'Power. Force. Fire. Energy. Magic,' Rayn replied. 'People have used different words, and the power can act in many ways.'

'What about trees and creatures and magical items?' Ada said, as they resumed walking towards the east.

'It's the same. It depends on how they were made, and how much power went into making them. A yew tree that's been nourished by the sun for three hundred years will be stronger than a young pine living in a dense forest for ten years. From strong materials, a skilled artisan can craft durable items. From materials possessing magical energies, an enchanter can imbue magical items.'

'So the sun is the source of all the power in the world?'

'Much, but not all. Every element is potent in its own way, but we depend mostly on the sun. Even underground there is power in abundance, from the Black Sun trapped under the mountains. The Black Sun always struggles to break free, and from its power are created the precious stones, as well as the underground races and monsters. The dwarves are strong because they were created from the pressure from the mountains above them. Some say diamonds are the remnants of dead dwarves, buried under the stones many thousands of years ago.'

Rayn was winded from trying to talk at the same time as she walked as fast as she could. They reached a new river and followed the north bank upstream.

'Did the Black Sun create the dead man chasing us?' Ada asked.

'No. I don't think so. The undead are not natural beings. They are made by someone, for some purpose.'

'What purpose?'

'That is decided by the one who makes them. But I'm quite certain the dead man chasing us was made to collect starfall shards.'

'Why?'

'Because starfall shards contain energy that can be used to create potent magic.'

Was that why I was able to create fire from my hands? Ada wondered. For a moment, she longed for the power she had felt surging through her body. 'How many stones are there?'

'Nobody knows. Most of them disappear in the sea. Some burn. Others get crushed into small fragments as they impact on a mountainside. Sometimes, they hit marshland or a forest, and shard. Other times, they crash into forests or marshland, and some shards can be dug out of the ground.'

'So, for every starfall, more fragments are made? Sooner or later, everyone will have their own shard. Or some lord or wizard will collect several shards, and grow stronger than everybody else?' Ada said.

'Yes, but only for a short time. It creates an imbalance. A disturbance, as too much power resides in one place or person. Some will use it to hoard treasure or destroy their enemies. Others will be envious of those who prosper, and seek to eliminate them or steal their shards. When shards are kept together, they interact with each other in unforeseen ways. There will be magical accidents when someone starts using magic far beyond their ability, and this many shards can break or burn out. People will die, and cities will burn.'

'Sounds dangerous,' Ada mused.

'Yes. That's why magic was banned.'

'How come you know all this?'

'How come you don't?' Rayn replied. 'Do you know how to read? Didn't you learn anything at the academy?'

Ada took a moment to consider the question. She never got the impression they had tried to teach anything at the academy, except that it was wrong and illegal to use magic. All she could remember from those years was the punishment and shame they had exerted on her. Then again, she hadn't really tried to learn anything. She was too busy drowning her shame and loneliness in the attention of others. That is where she met her first lover. And her tenth.

'I learned that I'm a useless hussy, I guess,' Ada said.

'That's only half true,' Rayn consoled.

Chapter 14: Straws

The dirt road was in poor condition and showed no signs of maintenance in recent years. Still, several fresh tracks from men and animals revealed that the road was in use. Ada and Rayn stood at a bend. One way led due south. The other followed the south bank of the river, towards the Jaw Mountains in the east.

'I'm going to die if I don't get to eat soon,' Ada said, pointing south. 'If there is a town nearby, we're more likely to find one in the lowlands than in the mountains.'

'Stop thinking with your feelings.' The half-elf had already walked a dozen steps on the eastbound road, indicating her preference.

'Hunger is not a feeling! It's a very real problem. People die of hunger.'

'In four days, hunger will be a problem. Today, it's an unpleasant feeling.'

'How come hunger is a feeling, but your weird obsession with a stone is a real problem?'

'Because the stone is part of me,' Rayn said.

'That's just silly.'

'No, it's not. We've bonded. If I lose the shard, I lose a part of myself.'

'Bah! That's even sillier!' Ada waved her arms in frustration.

'No. A fact is just silly because you don't understand. It's still a fact. Your ignorance is silly. You live your life feeling much and knowing little.'

'Right. Explain this to me then. Does everybody bond with any shiny bauble they fancy, or does it only apply to rude half-elves?' Ada asked.

'I'm the only one in Sandcastle.'

Ada snorted. 'Because you're so special?'

'Because I'm a crystal mage.'

Ada shook her head in disbelief. 'What is that?'

'Someone who works her magic by the use of stones, gems and crystals.'

'And you can do that?'

'Yes. How come you haven't noticed?' Rayn said.

Ada took a moment to consider the question. 'The healing salve? That was your crystal magic?'

'Yes, of course. That's part of it. Do you think you can just sprinkle a handful of sand on a burn wound and watch it heal within a few hours?'

'No, probably not,' Ada said.

'Good. I'm glad we talked. The shard has been carried to the east, somewhere not far from here. Let's go!' Rayn started walking up the road.

'No, wait!'

'Now what?' Rayn turned to look at her.

'Your being a crystal mage doesn't change anything. We still need food, and we'll freeze to death as soon as we stop walking.' Ada briefly examined what remained of her torn clothing. 'Besides, our clothes provide neither warmth nor privacy. If we walk into a mining town looking like this, we'll draw attention from all kinds of predators. You're even worse off than I.'

Rayn looked down at her nightgown and pulled at it lightly with her fingers. She nodded but did not seem overly concerned. 'As opposed to your warm and peaceful town to the south, I guess?'

Ada sighed. 'We'll draw straws.' She picked up two thick straws from the side of the road and broke them into unequal lengths. As she walked to Rayn, she tucked them into her fist, concealing one end of both.

Rayn pulled out what proved to be the shortest straw.

'I win!' Ada said, and started walking south with a smug smile on her face.

'No.'

'What?' Ada stopped and turned.

'We can't make important decisions based on luck or coincidence.'

'But you agreed! Why did you pick a straw if you never intended to follow me south if you lost?'

'Because there was a one in two chance you would stop whining,' The half-elf said, turning her back on Ada and resumed dragging her feet up the dirt road in the dark.

Chapter 15: Meeting

The following evening Gilmir and Hobble were waiting outside the same tunnel door Gilmir had emerged from. They had concealed themselves in the shadows of a large ash tree. The moon was up, and a few stars were already showing. The air was brisk.

The evening before Hobble had taken Gilmir to an inn and brought him food and wine. He had eaten well and managed to avoid complaining about the wine. The halfling had rented a room, and Gilmir slept in a bed for the first time in years—two years one hundred and sixty-nine days —to be precise. With the halfling's dagger, he had even cut his hair. Gilmir could not remember ever being in so much debt to another person.

When he woke, he felt better than he had done in months. He was not actively dying. Sure, he might as well be trapped in the gout-ridden body of an eighty-year-old human, but still. He felt *better*! That was all that mattered. If he improved every day, or most days, he would eventually regain his strength.

In some ways, it was fitting. If he was to start a new life, it was suitable that he started from scratch. In some ways that would be easier. Glancing at the halfling at his side, he wondered about the little guy's motives. Why had he helped him? Was he some sort of investment? That was the most likely explanation. If so, Hobble would guard his investment until it started to pay off. Or, until he lost faith in the project and decided to cut his losses. Either way, he expected to be safe until after they retrieved the starfall stone. After that, he would have to be on his guard.

Hobble nudged him with an elbow to his ribs. Gilmir came out of his reveries and followed the halfling's gaze. Dick and Shark emerged from the tunnel. They glanced around and started down the path heading south. Hobble waited until the two men were almost out of sight before he started after them. Gilmir let the halfling take the lead. Hobble showed himself to be a skilful stalker. With a slight shake of his head, Gilmir had to admit that even here, he played the part of the weakest link in the chain. At least the pace was measured, and he managed to follow without collapsing.

A quartermark later, they arrived at an abandoned farm. The two men stopped at the outskirts, beneath a great oak. Hobble crept up behind some bushes by the side of the path they had been following. It was a suitable spot. They would be hard to detect for any following the path or coming from the farm. Shark sat down by the oak. Dick did not stay still—pacing the clearing in front of the tree. Gilmir tapped Hobble on the shoulder, pointed to his eyes and into the forest, in the opposite direction from where Hobble was staring. Many a spy had lost their life staring at a target and not paying attention to their surroundings.

Hobble nudged him. 'Someone is coming,' he whispered.

Gilmir turned his head and saw a dwarf approaching from the farm. He wore a broad-brimmed hat cloaking his face in shadows. A dark grey beard fell down over his chest, and he carried an axe at his hip. Shark got to his feet and exchanged a few words with the newcomer. After that, the trade went fast. Shark handed over a pouch and got something wrapped in cloth in return. Gilmir turned his gaze towards the forest again.

'Okay, they have the stone, and we can go about getting it,' Hobble whispered. 'They are two, so I need a distraction. Remember the clearing where the path went by that boulder?'

Gilmir nodded.

'Good, good. Do you think you can get there ahead of them and meet them from the other side?'

'I think so,' Gilmir said and started planning a route through the forest. 'What do you need me to do?'

'Oh, no, nothin' much. I just need a distraction for a moment. Walk up—ask a question or somethin'.'

Gilmir started off. Soon, he entered the clearing where the boulder sat in the middle. He was short of breath, and sweat ran down his chin. The two men in front of him stopped. Dick twitched and laid a hand on the hilt of the sword hanging from his belt. Shark only smiled showing his crooked teeth.

'Good evening, master.'

'Good evening to you, fine sirs,' Gilmir replied. He did not leave the path but stopped in front of the two men.

'Can we help you with something?' Shark asked.

'I suspect you can, Shark. Please tell me where this path leads,' Gilmir said and made an exaggerated movement with his arm, pointing up and down the trail.

'Sorry, I think you confuse me with someone else,' Shark said, while Hobble crept up in position behind him.

Gilmir shook his head. 'Oh, no, I don't think so!' He looked down the path in the direction he came from. 'You see, I lost my friend's trail somewhere down there. And now you are coming here, I would say you are defiantly the one I am looking for.'

Behind the man, Hobble seemed to finish his work. With a nod to Gilmir, he disappeared behind the boulder.

'*Definitely*, you mean.'

'Oh no, sir, she is called Beatrice, and she is a lovely specimen.'

The two men glanced at each other. 'Best of luck finding your friend,' Shark said and started past him. 'You sick bastard,' he added in a mumble.

Gilmir smiled and let the two men pass. He stood watching them disappearing down the trail, before he returned to Hobble behind the boulder. Together, they walked into the forest. After a while, Hobble stopped and gave Gilmir the cloth-wrapped object. The elf opened the package with trembling hands. He took the stone in his hand, a smile spreading across his face. The shard was dark grey, with spots of red and silver. And a little larger than his thumb. This was what he needed, this stone would give him strength. Life. Power. With this he could start his new life.

His smile fell away while he lifted his gaze slightly and found Hobble's eyes. 'Why did you let them go?'

'Let them go? You have the stone haven't you?'

'I do. But what do you think the two thugs are going to do when they find the stone missing?'

'They won't. Not for a while, at least. They have another stone.'

'One looking like this?' Gilmir held up his hand displaying the shard.

'No, of course not, I didn't know the exact appearance of the shard. But they have a stone, and will probably not find out for some time.'

'I assumed you needed a distraction so you could take them out. Leaving such loose ends is …' He trailed off when he saw the expression on Hobble's face.

'Did you think I was going to kill them for you? Kill two people to give you that stone? Do you realise how insane that is!?'

Gilmir did not respond. He stared down at the halfling. After several moments he broke out in a smile. 'Nah, I'm jesting, you did a fine job there.' He clapped Hobble on the shoulder. 'Let's head back to town.'

The halfling started limping away, supported by his staff. His left foot, which appeared fine a moment before, was once again bent at the ankle.

Chapter 16: Rider

The biting wind from the Jaw Mountains was growing stronger. Only fear of lurking predators kept the two miserable women going through the night.

Ada put her hand around Rayn and tried to summon enough warmth to sustain them both. At first, the effort felt like drinking water from a bucket of sand. There was nothing. She felt spent but made another attempt at absorbing what little heat could be extracted from her surroundings. This time it worked, albeit slowly. Warmth spread from deep within her, as if she had been drinking a cup of hot tea.

Rayn shivered and pulled away. 'Stop it! You're making it worse.'

'I'm sorry,' Ada said, embarrassed as she realised that she had used her friend as the involuntary source of heat.

'You have no focus.'

'What do you mean?'

'Have you seen what happens when the sun shines through a magnifying glass?' Rayn asked.

'Of course. The sunlight is focused and burns hotter.'

'That's right. With you, it's the other way around. You require extraordinary amounts of heat to work the simplest of spells.'

'Not true! I did quite well against the intruder last night.'

'Yes, I noticed. But you were all but sitting in a fireplace, half aflame, and the urgency of the situation might have forced you to focus.'

'I'm sorry. I have no training, so I don't know how to focus.'

Rayn didn't reply. She kept to the left side of the road, hugging herself as she walked.

'Can you teach me how to use fire magic?' Ada asked.

'No. I don't know much about elemental magic.'

'Can you teach me how to be a crystal mage, then?'

Rayn snorted. 'I could. But it would be a waste of time.'

'Why?'

'Because you clearly have an affinity for the elements, not stones. With training, you would make a decent elementalist, but no more than a mediocre crystal mage peddling worthless crystals and ineffective salves in the streets,' Rayn said.

'Crystal mages do that?'

'Some, I guess. As would some shamans, alchemists and enchanters with little training or experience, never developing their abilities beyond the most basic.'

'I had no idea the street peddlers knew magic. I thought they were all hustlers and con artists.'

'There are those, too. But if they were all swindlers, nobody would buy their wares. People buy a rabbit's foot because they sometimes work.'

Ada laughed. 'Surely, they don't.'

'They do. When properly imbued with the spirit of the animal, a rabbit's foot will sometimes bring luck. A well-prepared potion might cure a child ridden with pox. Even love potions might work, when done right. That's why people keep buying them.'

'I never knew that.'

'Someone's coming,' Rayn whispered.

'What?' Ada turned to look behind but saw nobody. She peered into the darkness ahead. 'Where? I don't see anybody.'

Rayn was gone.

'Rayn? Rayn! Where are you?'

Then she heard the hoof steps. Too close. Ada briefly considered jumping into the nearby bushes but did not care enough to make the effort. She carried nothing of value, and she could not imagine anyone would take an interest in killing or abducting her.

She regretted the decision as soon as the cloaked rider appeared, reining in his horse a few feet away. His red eyes found hers, lingering for two or three heartbeats before they started scanning her surroundings.

Ada froze. She had never seen red eyes before, and she did not know what it meant. But she was sure it was not a good sign. 'Move along, or my friends will release their arrows!'

The rider uttered an unfamiliar sound from underneath his hood and pinned her with his scarlet gaze. 'You have but one friend, who would already be dead if she carried a bow or any other weapon.'

The rider spoke with an alien accent, his voice smooth and cold as melting ice. Frightening and alluring, with the calm and assured demeanour of one who truly believed he was superior to anyone and anything.

As if boosted by the stranger's confidence, Ada found her own courage. 'Where is the nearest town?'

In the silence that followed, Ada examined the rider. He was shorter than most men, and the wet cloak clung to narrow shoulders. Underneath the oversized hood, he'd wrapped a scarf around his head and neck, fully covering his face below his eyes.

'Up there,' he said, almost in a whisper. He nodded slightly, in the direction they had been walking.

Ada turned and peered towards the east. If there was a town nearby, she would expect to see some lights. But there was nothing. 'Is it far?'

'Not far …' the rider replied.

'Take me with you!' Ada said, and instantly regretted the blatant honesty of the request. 'I mean *us*. Take us to the town, before the predators chase us down in the night.'

The rider made the strange sound again, longer and louder this time. A laugh, although different from any Ada had ever heard.

'Worry not about the dangers of the road, girl. If you enter Sha'ton tonight, you'll find yourself on your back entertaining a pack of predators before dawn.'

'But we'll freeze to death if we can't find shelter!' she protested, somehow feeling hurt by the stranger's indifference.

'There are many ways to die, girl. Freezing to death is preferable to most.'

Tears welled up in Ada's eyes. 'How can you be so cold?'

The rider tugged the reins lightly, and the horse started trotting towards the east.

'If you'd seen what I've seen, you would be cold too. One way or the other.'

Chapter 17: Fight

Gilmir and Hobble almost managed to get to Shacktown before Gilmir slumped to the ground. Clouds gathered in the darkening sky, and the wind picked up. They were at the outskirts of the city's graveyard, and Gilmir put his back against a mausoleum wall. Hobble stood over him, leaning on his staff.

'That stone did not help you much, did it? What's it supposed to do?' Hobble asked.

'It will help, but it is not an instant cure,' Gilmir said, ignoring his companion's second question.

'Guess you need food, water and rest. Or is it something more? Are you hurt? Diseased? Poisoned?'

'Some old wounds, but nothing serious. I think you are right. Some rest, food and wine—fine wine—should fix this. How about you, what is the trick with your foot? Can you deform it at—'

Gilmir broke off his questions and indicated for Hobble to be silent. He strained his ears. Something was coming. Through the woods. With heavy steps. It was moving like a charging bull but without the speed. Going straight through bushes and branches.

'Someone is coming. Or something.' He nodded towards the woods. Hobble turned and lifted his staff.

Out of the bushes came a man stumbling. No, not a man, a corpse. Tatters of old clothing hung on him seemingly at random, pale skin bared beneath. His left arm hung limp, probably because of the deep cut below the shoulder. Across his chest, a vicious wound displayed white bones and red-blooded flesh. The living dead came straight towards them.

Hobble rushed forward on quick feet and cracked the staff against the creature's head, leaving a dent in its skull. The corpse stopped for a moment as if to consider the consequences of the blow. It started forward again, swinging its right arm at the halfling. Hobble jumped back and swung his staff again. This time it hit the already limp arm, not even slowing the creature.

Hobble connected blow after blow, to no effect, and the living dead kept swinging after the agile halfling who kept dodging.

'Go for his knees!' Gilmir, shouted. Hobble would soon tire and the creature would eventually land one of its heavy blows and the fight would be over. Hobble would have to cripple him. Gilmir saw the halfling redirecting his strikes. He landed a blow to the side of the corpse's knee but nothing happened. This would not end well.

The two combatants came close to the wall where Gilmir stood, and Hobble moved a few steps to the side. The undead did not follow. Instead, it continued towards Gilmir and swung at him. Gilmir dodged, and kicked at the creature's knee. The blow landed solidly, but to no avail. He did not have the strength to damage the joint with a kick.

'Hit it!' Gilmir shouted to Hobble. The halfling would tire fast, but Gilmir was not sure he could even evade a few more blows before exhaustion retook him. No help came. He dodged another swing. The halfling was nowhere to be seen. Had he abandoned him? Had he finally cut his losses and left him to deal with the living dead, escaping while the creature was occupied with another victim? It was the wise thing to do. It was what he would have done …

Crack.

Hidden from view by the dead man, Hobble smashed his staff into the creature's knee. It buckled. Stopped. Straightened up, and turned.

At least Gilmir was safe for a moment. 'You must strike harder!'

'Really?' Hobble jumped. 'Why …'—Hobble took another swing—'didn't I …'—then dodged —'think …'—backstepped—'of …'—and sidestepped before taking a final swing—'that!'

This time, the blow hit the creature's thigh. To no effect. In the background, two figures emerged from the woods where the creature had come from. Two women, in similarly ragged clothes, dirty skin showing underneath. *Balls! More bloody, walking corpses!*

Gilmir closed his eyes. There was no way to escape three of the accursed beasts.

'Hit his knees!' one of the newly arrived corpses shouted. *Shouting corpses now?* He opened his eyes. The two women were not dead. They were two of the most sorry-looking beings he had ever seen … Well, at least since he had glimpsed himself in the reflection of the water the day he came out from the sewers. Now the two women were cheering Hobble on.

Once again, the wind picked up and shook in the nearby trees. One of the women shouted something. Hobble danced and jumped. Leaves whirled up from the ground, branches whipped about. Gilmir shielded his eyes. The howling of the wind cancelled out every other sound. Grass, leaves and sand kept spiralling in towards the spot where Hobble and the living dead were fighting. Tighter and tighter, closer and closer. Abruptly, it stopped.

Hobble struck with his staff. Once, twice, three times, in rapid succession. Like strikes of lightning. The sound of cracking bones and dislocating joints followed each blow. The living corpse fell to the ground, unable to stand, unable to swing his mighty blows. In the next moment, Hobble dropped to his knees, breathing hard. The two women did the same. All three were exhausted. There was no sound, no wind, no movement. Everything was still.

The living dead started moving again. It dragged itself over the ground, using its broken arms to pull, and its shattered feet to push. Gilmir rose. He went over to Hobble and took the knife the halfling wore at his belt. The elf walked over to the living dead, placed one foot on the creature's back and pushed it to the ground. His eyes scanned the body and soon found what he was looking for. Bending down, he stabbed the knife into the creature's neck. He worked it from side to side for a moment and then plunged his hand into the wound.

Chapter 18: Shards

Gilmir extended his arm and unclenched his fist, revealing a blood-smeared, black stone, about the size of his thumb. He waited for Hobble and the two young women to get back on their feet and gather around him. They unceremoniously exchanged names, before switching attention to the stone in the elf's hand.

'Another stone from the starfall,' Gilmir said, and reached for the shard he kept in his pocket. As he held one in each hand next to each other, a high-pitched sound emanated, and the shards started vibrating in his hand.

'What's that noise?' Hobble asked.

'The shards are talking to each other. They are kin, ever connected,' said Rayn. She walked the four steps to the now unmoving corpse and searched what remained of his clothing. Beats later, she was back by Gilmir's side, holding two more shards, one in each hand. The stone in her left palm was attached to a chain, like a pendant. The noise intensified, like a choir of distressed rodents. 'It is not wise to keep them together. The interference is unpredictable, and sooner or later, there will be accidents.'

'What kind of accidents?' Hobble glanced from Rayn to Gilmir.

'Loss of limbs, loss of lives,' Gilmir said. 'Madness. Fires. Thunderstorms. Rampaging demons.'

'Demons?' Ada said. 'What are those?'

'Essences,' Gilmir replied. 'Spirits from other planes. When they are called to our world by some overly eager human summoner, they take physical forms that might be monstrous. Most possess magical powers as well, and they make formidable foes. Such beings invariably cause havoc.'

'That's why we keep them apart,' Rayn said, and hung the shard pendant around her neck. The other stone she gave to Ada. 'Take this. I believe it has chosen you.'

Ada accepted the gift with a solemn nod. Holding the shard in one hand, she ran a thumb slowly over the smooth surface, caressing it.

'What do we do with this?' Gilmir asked.

Rayn examined the shard, and frowned. 'It's tainted. We should destroy it.'

'What do you mean?' replied Hobble.

'It's imbued with some minor spirit and combined with an animated corpse to create that,' Rayn pointed towards the corpse on the ground.

'What kind of spirit?' asked Hobble.

'I need more time to know for sure. A stubborn animal, possibly a ram or a boar, or even a badger.' Rayn nodded, apparently satisfied with her reasoning.

'Ah, give me that!' Hobble picked the shard from Rayn's hand, and clutched it in his fist.

'Stop it, halfling! Don't be stupid. We must destroy the stone before it messes things up.' Gilmir reached for the shard.

'No chance.' Hobble evaded the feeble attempt at taking the shard by force. 'You all got one, and I'm keeping this. It's valuable, and I'm not destroying it just because you're afraid of some badger demon.'

'Besides, *you* owe me.' Hobble looked pointedly at Gilmir.

Ada broke the silence. 'While you boys are having a staring contest, I'm dying of thirst over here. Anyone have something to drink?'

Hobble cleared his throat, and took a satchel from his back. Seeming happy to end the stare-off, he sat down on one knee. He pulled a bottle of wine from the bag.

'Hungry? I have some bread and cheese too.'

'Yes, please!' Ada replied.

Soon, the new companions sat sharing the small meal.

'So, what are the two of you doing here?' Hobble asked.

Ada and Rayn shared a look.

'Isn't it obvious?' Rayn said.

'He was trying to be polite,' Gilmir said, giving Rayn a look, 'It is of course no coincidence. The dead man had your pendant and you were following it. But from where? And how did he get hold of the pendant?'

Rayn was about to answer but Ada lay a hand on her forearm.

'We're from Sandcastle. That monster attacked us in Rayn's shop. We ran, and it followed. In the end, we had to let it have it. Afterwards we followed it here.'

'So it did not care about you after it got hold of the stone?' Gilmir said.

'No,' Ada said.

Gilmir pondered the new information.

'So what are you going to do now?' Hobble asked.

'With that monster dead, I think we'll head home.' Ada replied.

'Not tonight, obviously,' Rayn said.

'The danger is not over. I am sorry to say,' Gilmir responded.

'What do you mean?' Ada asked.

'Someone is collecting these stones. And it was not the dead man's idea. Someone created it for that purpose. That someone will not stop with this.'

Rayn and Ada shared a look again.

Gilmir continued. 'I think I know who it is. Give me a few days and I will know for sure.'

'And then what?' Rayn asked.

'If you want to keep those stones, we will have to do something about it. And we probably should stay together until then.'

'No,' Rayn said abruptly. The three others looked at the half-elf.

When no explanation was forthcoming, Gilmir said, 'No, what?'

'No, we are not coming with you. And we are not "going to do something about it". We are going home. Tomorrow.'

Ada started to protest. 'But, Rayn—'

'No!' Rayn cut her short. 'You would trust any man—male—and I will not let you make this decision. Besides, having four shards that close together is not a good idea.' She looked at Gilmir. 'And I am not staying nearby that evil shard!' She nodded toward Hobble.

Ada looked at Gilmir and shrugged with an apologetic expression.

After that, they ate in silence for a while.

'If you change your mind, we are staying at The Pick and the Axe in Oldtown,' Hobble said, while putting the empty wine bottle back in the satchel.

Chapter 19: Thugs

'Now what?' Ada asked, as she watched the elf and the halfling disappear under the stone arches that once had been part of the city gates.

Rayn didn't answer. Instead, she slumped down against an old tombstone and closed her eyes. Ada joined her, and for some time, neither of them uttered a single word. This was the first break or respite since they fled from the inn at Bargetown at noon the day before. Exhaustion overcame them, and they slept until shouting voices woke them up.

'I'll break every bone in your puny, piece of shit body!'

Ada opened her eyes, instantly awake. She reached for something but realised she carried nothing to use for defence. Not even the knife she always kept strapped by her hip in the streets of Sandcastle. By her side, Rayn also stirred, but both remained seated on the ground with their backs against the stone.

The graveyard was different in the daylight. From where they were sitting, there appeared to be no order or system to it. New graves nestled between old ones, and statues, tombstones and small mausoleums cast shadows that created hiding places for anyone who did not want to be found.

One such person, a scrawny boy of about twelve, darted between the stones some twenty yards away. Soon, three other boys, bigger and most likely older, appeared.

'Fine, I won't hurt you. Just give me the damn necklace, and you're free to go as you please,' the larger of them shouted. He was almost as tall as a man.

'I wouldn't take him up on his offer, if I was you,' Ada whispered.

The boy froze as if he heard her. His eyes met Ada's, and he lifted his finger to his lips, pleading.

'Hey, girls!' The older boys spotted the women and walked quickly to stand before them. They were all doing their best to appear as menacing as possible, with smug smiles and puffed chests.

'You smell of sewage, boys. Go home and have your mama change your diapers,' Ada dismissed them.

The insult apparently made the pack forget about the boy they chased. The larger boy's fake smile melted like wax on a hot stove, only to be replaced by a far more sinister expression. One a young woman growing up in the streets of Sandcastle knew all too well.

The boy made a show of grabbing his crotch and looking at his compatriots for support and confirmation.

'I know what you're going to smell of when we're finished with you,' he said.

'Good for you!' Ada forced herself to laugh despite her fear. She regretted her approach to the young thugs, but there was no going back. 'You can fantasise about that when you fondle each other tonight.'

'You've got a filthy mouth on you, whore! But I know how to silence you.' He grinned and pulled down his pants to reveal his excitement at the prospect.

Ada laughed again and pointed to the corpse that had been chasing them the day before. It lay face down in the mud a dozen steps to their right, its broken skull clearly visible. 'That guy said the same thing last night. His was much bigger, though. He was a grown man, not a boy of twelve like yourself.'

'I'm sixteen!' the boy protested, looking at the mutilated corpse. After a moment, a smile started to spread across his face. 'That man has been dead for weeks! I watched him die in the arena at the full moon festival!' The thug started toward Ada again.

Rayn pulled on Ada's arm. 'Let's go! Even I know that look!'

'I can't back down!' Ada whispered to Rayn, and pulled free. 'Not this time.'

The boy closed in with his trousers around his knees. His smile was replaced by an evil grin. The other brats hooted and shouted encouragement to their sinister champion. Ada did not know what to expect but prepared as best she could.

The boy's arms shot out faster than anticipated. He took hold of the front of Ada's shirt, or what was left of it, and tugged her forward and down. She fell to her knees in front of him, the shirt pulled halfway over her face and his fist pressed against her cheeks. Ada seized his wrists and tried to focus her mind.

The boy smiled down at her and raised an eyebrow. 'Let go and it will hurt less.'

Ada tried to channel heat through her hands. It did not work. She had no fire to draw thermal energy from. She let go of his wrists.

Rayn shouted and came forward, but the other boys caught her. Laughter and jeers filled Ada's ears. How tired she was of being bullied, hunted and assaulted. Sick of men, dead men and boys thinking they could do what they wanted with her.

Warmth started spreading in her belly. That other kind of fire. Fuelled by anger and despair.

The thug took her by the hair and started pulling her further down. More fuel for the fire.

Ada channelled the warmth from the belly, through her chest, via her right shoulder and down her arm. She did not need two hands for this job. Sensing the warmth emanating from her hand like a torch, she knew she was ready.

Ada plunged her hand between the boy's legs. Taking hold of his sack, she squeezed. The sizzling silenced all other noise. For several beats all was still. At last the boy's body felt what his dim wit could not comprehend.

He screamed.

The thugs surrounding them, stared with open mouths.

'Piss off before I really get angry!' Ada said, letting go of the scalded sack.

The thug turned and tried to run with his hands on his groin and his pants around his knees. He fell.

The rest of the gang backed off, mumbling words like 'sorcery', 'witch' and 'magic'.

The burnt boy crawled to his feet. Pulling at his trousers, he jumped more than he ran. 'Stay away from me, you crazy witch!'

Ada watched the thugs run off before she leaned back against the tombstone, closing her eyes. She felt Rayn slump down beside her.

'Calls of witches and sorcery, are seldom good signs,' Rayn said.

'Not even for the witches?' Ada replied, while her eyes remained closed.

'Especially not for the witches.'

Chapter 20: Understanding

'I'll deduct one from my debt to you for that one.' Gilmir nodded towards the stone Hobble held in his open palm. 'Now, put it away. You don't flaunt those around.'

'So, you only owe me for five of the six times I saved your life?' Hobble responded, and put away the stone.

'Six now, right?'

'Mhm. One for getting you out of the cell.' Hobble held his thumb up. 'One for dragging you out of the sewer you were drowning in, and one for coming back and telling you not to go for the swim. That makes three.' Hobble showed two more fingers. 'Then we have the food, the wine, the bed. I'll be gracious and count one for all that. The stone counts for one, and then we have that abomination, which clearly came for you and not me.' The halfling held up six short fingers, wiggling them in front of Gilmir.

Gilmir sighed and shook his head. They continued in silence for a moment, before Gilmir spoke.

'About the living dead. You did a decent job. But I don't understand this. You struck him three dozen times, and I told you to strike harder. To no avail. But then, the two girls came and told you the same. And behold! You all but disassembled the monstrosity in three strikes. All you needed was a girl cheering you on?'

Hobble gazed to his staff, which he still used as support for his left foot—once again deformed. 'There was more than that.'

'What do you mean?' Gilmir asked, needing to confirm his suspicions.

'It was just like the wind gathered in the staff. Making it lighter, easier to swing, but still harder, and more substantial. All came from the girl. I could feel it.' Hobble glanced up, meeting Gilmir's eyes. The halfling looked terrified.

'Some mighty elemental magic, for a little girl,' Gilmir said, 'and that was before she had the shard.'

'The stone helps with that sort of thing? Can you do that?'

'Yes and no. The stone intensifies magical powers,' Gilmir said, before he changed the subject. 'How does the staff feel now?'

Hobble hefted the staff in his hand. 'It still feels light and … different. It feels different.'

'Is it silver oak?'

'Some kind of oak I think, yes. Why?'

'Silver oak has the capacity to store magic. Quite possibly, the staff is now imbued with wind magic.'

Hobble lifted the staff and studied it intently. 'Forever?'

'Impossible to say. It may last a day, a week, a month or even years. I am not completely sure the girl knew what she was doing.'

They walked in silence as they came to the miners' quarter. The name was a remnant from the time the city had been a mining town. Now it was a shabby part of the old town, although with sturdy brick houses and not the rickety wooden buildings of the newer parts of the city.

'Here, I almost forgot,' Gilmir held out the knife he had borrowed at the end of the fight with the living dead.

'Nah, you keep it. You'll need a weapon. Besides, you seem to know how to handle a knife.'

Gilmir had to smile at the remark. 'Thank you.'

The sign for The Pick and the Axe came into view. The inn they had stayed in last night.

'Now, listen,' Hobble said, 'I have the coin for a few nights with food, wine and a roof over our head. But you'll need to pay off your share until the day you've made it worth my while. Capeesh?'

Gilmir nodded as they walked through the door of the inn. Knowing all too well that the situation was much more dire than lacking money for food and a room.

Chapter 21: Bets

At midday, the two sparsely dressed women walked through the main street of Sha'ton. There were no guards, no patrols, nothing indicating the presence of law enforcement in the city. What had once been a city wall had long since collapsed. Ramshackle wooden houses and bridges had been built on top of and between the old stone buildings. Now, they were all leaning against each other, giving the impression of a tunnel that might collapse any time.

Despite their best efforts at covering as much skin as possible with their tattered clothes, the rider's warning about the town's predators seemed accurate. Hungry eyes measured them up and down as they passed.

'We need new clothes,' Ada said.

'And food,' Rayn added.

'Yes, of course,' Ada said, not revealing her suspicion that they would probably not survive long enough for lack of food to be a concern. 'And then we go home.'

'Which home? My home burned to the ground.'

'You can't be certain.'

'Yes, I am.'

Ada sighed. 'We stand a better chance in the streets of Sandcastle, or even in the woods, than in this place.'

'But how do we find food and clothes here?'

'I don't know yet, but I'll find a way.'

They kept to the streets and open places, fearing what might befall them if they were cornered in a deserted alley. Other women walked the streets. Most plain, dressed in unflattering threadbare tunics, who failed to draw anyone's attention. There were also the beauties: the nobleman's daughter, or rich man's escort, wearing silk dresses that barely covered the bottom third of their breasts. They attracted plenty of stares as they moved as gracefully as was possible in the muddy streets, but nobody seemed to approach them or utter a single unsavoury remark.

A dozen dwarves, a handful of gnomes and a pair of elves added to the mostly human population in the streets. As well as a couple of humanoids Ada had never seen or heard of before. Children played in the streets like in any other city. But their games were different from the games most children play.

The children of Sha'ton were fighting.

Whenever they encountered a group of kids, usually boys, at least two of them would be fighting while the others cheered. As they passed one of those groups, a subtle sensation of familiarity made Ada stop. She gently pulled Rayn's arm to get her attention. 'Come, I want to see this.'

They approached the makeshift arena. A stone ring, ten or twelve steps wide, surrounded the broken remains of a fountain. An audience of twenty, children and adults alike, cheered as two boys tangled on the stone. The larger of the two had the smaller boy's head locked under his right arm, and used his left to tighten the vice even harder.

Ada had seen enough fighting to know that the contest was all but over at that point.

'Choke him! Squeeze his head off!' the man beside her shouted.

When Ada turned to establish what kind of person would encourage children to kill each other, she noticed the source of their enthusiasm. The audience made bets on the outcome of the fight, and the blood-thirsty man who had called for the end of the smaller boy's life opened a leather pouch to increase his stake.

A loud collective groan went up as the smaller boy drove his elbow into his opponent's groin. As usual, a brief pause ensued until the unfortunate boy felt the full effect of the punch. But then, his grip around his opponent's head loosened, and his victim managed to break free.

In the excitement, Ada stepped on a loose stone, tripped and fell against the brutal man next to her. He unceremoniously brushed her aside, causing her to land in the ring. Someone grabbed her by the upper arm and pulled her out, and Ada scrambled to her feet and found her place in the crowd. The hard fall gave her another couple of scrapes and bruises, to go with the dozens she got the day before. More importantly, it had provided her with the opportunity to pilfer some coins from the oblivious brute next to hear.

Biting back the pain, she found a young man taking bets on the fight. He had shaved the sides of his head, leaving a stripe of inch-long, blond hair in the middle. His chin displayed a pathetic parody of a beard.

'Two bits on the little one,' Ada said and produced two triangular metal pieces from her closed hand.

The bookmaker could not hide a smile as he accepted her bits and handed her two green-dyed strips of leather that confirmed the bet.

As she returned to her spot next to Rayn, she couldn't help but notice that everybody else was waving red strips of leather as they cheered their chosen fighter in the arena.

'That's the boy from last night,' Rayn said.

'Sure is,' Ada confirmed, looking at the smaller boy who was savouring the opportunity to breathe after he had broken free from the headlock. There was a desperation in his eyes, an urge to win that was stronger than any fear of taking on someone two or three years older than himself.

The boy made no attempt at attacking his prone opponent, who was still trying to recover from the blow to his most sensitives. Instead, he put his hands on his knees and breathed deeply, preparing for what was to come.

When the larger boy got to his feet and charged, the scrawny kid was ready.

He grabbed his opponent's right arm and shoulder and turned his hip and back to meet the impact. Using the momentum of the reckless charge, he sent the body in a vertical arc over his shoulder. There was a soft thud as the elder boy landed flat on his back, forcing the air out of his lungs.

The smaller boy still kept hold of his unfortunate opponent's right arm, and now he twisted it slowly for additional effect. Shouting insults, the audience threw their red leather strips in the ring. The fight was over.

As the crowd dispersed, Ada exchanged her two green strips for eight bits of silver.

Chapter 22: Scheme

Gilmir spent most of the day eating and sleeping. He needed much of both. Hobble was out and about for hours, and they did not see each other much until evening. After sundown, they sat in the inn's common room sharing a bowl of stew and a bottle of wine. Gilmir sat with his back against the wall, in one corner of the room. From where he sat, he could keep an eye on the door, the counter, and the stairs to the second floor where they had their room. From the other side of the table, Hobble yawned.

'Tired?' Gilmir asked.

'Yeah, I didn't sleep well last night. I kept dreaming about shards 'n' stones 'n' falling stars.'

The door went up, and a dwarf walked in. He had black hair and a beard. A wolf pelt lay over his shoulders, and he wore leather trousers and mail armour. On his back, he carried a giant axe and a backpack. In his belt, several knives hung and a wand stuck out. He wore rings on most fingers and a pendant around his neck. The newcomer scanned the room. He moved to a free table where he dumped the axe and the backpack before he slumped down in a chair.

Hobble seemed to realise something caught Gilmir's attention and turned. Spinning back, he slid his chair back. 'I'll sit by your side. Can't see anythin' from over here.' He rose and came around the table, sitting down in a chair beside the elf.

'That is just silly,' Gilmir responded, 'we can't both sit on the same side.'

'Feel free to move,' Hobble said, stretching his short legs out under the table.

Gilmir considered it but decided he would rather be uncomfortable than have his back turned to the entire room.

'Who's that?' Hobble asked in a low voice, as if he was talking to himself, his eyes resting on the dwarf.

'I don't know. Probably some kind of treasure hunter coming back to town.'

'How you figure?'

'The rings, the pendant, the wand: he is no soldier. The large axe, which I reckon he knows how to use, is battle-worn, but well tended. The road dust on his clothes, the mud on his boots. Just my guess.'

'Let's go have a chat.' Hobble was already on his feet, limping towards the dwarf's table.

Slowly, feeling all his aches, Gilmir followed the halfling. The thief was right about one thing; the dwarf was the most interesting figure at the inn.

'Had I had the coin, I would buy you a beer, master dwarf,' Hobble said, pulling out a chair.

'I can buy my own ale, thank you, short one,' the dwarf replied, glancing at Hobble before he slapped a coin purse on the table and gestured for the serving girl.

'Do you mind if I pull up a chair, soldier?' Gilmir said.

'Suit yourself, tall one, there aren't many rules in Sha'ton. Even an elf is free to do almost as he pleases.' The dwarf looked him over before he added, 'Almost.'

Gilmir ignored the comment and took a seat.

'Besides, I haven't been a soldier for a half a century,' the dwarf said.

'So what do you do for a living?' Hobble asked.

'I am a collector,' the dwarf replied. 'Yeah, and before you ask. I collect trophies, artefacts, missing items, art, pendants, weapons, almost anything valuable.' He waved for the serving girl. 'Yes, yes, I'm careful.'

Hobble shot Gilmir a glance. Gilmir could not tell if the look was triggered by something the dwarf listed or if the last statement caused it.

'I am Hobble, and this is Gilmir.'

'Tracks,' the dwarf said while glancing around the room.

'So how is business these days in the collector trade?' Hobble asked.

'Not bad, not sad,' Tracks replied, before ordering food and beer from the serving girl. He placed his backpack under the table and leaned the axe against the wall. All the time, his mouth kept moving, and a muttering escaped his lips.

'I guess the starfall changed the playing field?' Hobble pressed on with his questions.

The dwarf glanced at Hobble. His mouth stopped moving, and his eyes shone with a new intensity. To Hobble's credit, he kept Tracks's gaze. For long moments, the two stared at each other. Gilmir studied the dwarf. He still looked into Hobble's eyes, as if he tried to read his soul. Suddenly, his mouth started moving again. No words, just mumbles. His hand went to a pouch on his belt. Then he turned away, shifting his gaze towards the bar. 'Where's that food and drink?'

Hobble shot Gilmir a look. Gilmir gave a tiny shake of his head in response. He was not sure what the halfling had been asking, but he was sure about the answer. Hobble needed to back off. The dwarf appeared dangerous and unstable. The worst combination of features he knew. Except for lovesick giants. And drunk female trolls. Either way, Hobble needed to back off. The halfling had turned his gaze towards the dwarf again.

'Why you call yourself Tracks?'

Gilmir exhaled.

'I don't, or at least, I didn't. An old friend of mine started calling me that. And it stuck. It seems I can be quiet and hard to find when I want, but he kept telling me I always leave tracks. At first, there was only him calling me so. Later, others started too. Soon everyone called me that. Nowadays, no one knows me by any other name.'

'There are worse things to be called,' Gilmir said.

'You speak truth there, elf!'

With that, the trio went silent for a while. Soon the serving girl came with food and ale for the dwarf. Tracks gave the girl some coins and said, 'Thank you, Chris!'

Chris smiled, curtsied and turned, hurrying off.

Gilmir followed the girl with his gaze. Her hand had given him pause. She was young, even by human standards. Her movements were quick and sure, navigating the busy room with confidence. A leather bracelet hung loose on her slender wrist, and brown hair fell to her shoulders. Her red dress was faded, and a broad leather belt went almost two rounds around her waist. The hand had been calloused.

Soon after, Gilmir and Hobble said their farewells to Tracks and went back to their room. They had little coin to spend, and Gilmir still needed lots of rest. Back in their small second-floor room, Gilmir lay down on his bed, crossing his arms under his head. Hobble sat down in a chair by the small window. He put his short legs on the table, leaned back and stared out on the darkening sky.

'We need money,' the halfling said.

'Yeah,' Gilmir said, and yawned.

'How?'

'How do you usually earn your living?' Gilmir closed his eyes.

'Lately, I have been fighting in the arena.'

'How is that working out for you?'

'I earn some since I am a club-footed halfling.'

'You mean you earn some because others underestimate you while you pretend to have a deformed foot?'

'Yeah.'

'How much do you earn?' Gilmir asked.

'It's the "Bits Arena", so just a few bits each match. Lately, I have been winning too often, so I might have to move on to one of the other arenas.'

'What's the next step?'

'Hmm, probably "the Rock" in the old mining tunnels, or the "Cage Arena" by the south gate.'

'Do you fight the arenas for money?'

'Yes, why else?' Hobble said, flicking a coin into the air with his thumb and catching it again.

'Perhaps you should lose some matches first. That way we can earn more by playing the underdog later.'

'We?'

'I can bet on you.'

'Ah, I see. So *I* can get my firm, little ass kicked for a few matches, so that *you* can use *my* coins to bet that I will eventually win a match. *I* will risk my health, my reputation and my handsome face AND my coin … And *your* contribution to this team effort would be?'

'I am obviously the brains behind the operation.' Gilmir tapped his temple, his eyes still closed. 'And I will earn the coin by betting against you in the first few matches and then investing handsomely in your victory later! It is a two-player scheme. Both parts are essential. It's not my fault that you have a deformed foot. You fit the part like a sword in an orc's heart. And, I can pull off being a gambler. I have done worse.'

Hobble did not answer, but Gilmir could feel his stare. He tried not to smile. After a few moments, he broke the silence. 'We can land the final details of the plan tomorrow. Good night, champion!'

Gilmir turned on his side and fell asleep with a smile on his face.

Chapter 23: Presence

The porridge was bland but warm. It served its purpose. So did the second-hand woollen tunics and pants they wore. They even had a generous chunk of bread for the road, but that was as far as their arena earnings had lasted.

'How do we find a place to live, and how do we find food when we get home?' Rayn's face was a mask of despair and frustration. She was as streetwise as a butterfly and would survive as long if left on her own in such circumstances.

'I'll find a way,' Ada said, 'I've lived on the streets for many years.'

'I refuse to move in with one of your useless boyfriends!' The idea seemed to frighten Rayn more than anything. Her face reddened, and her pitch was higher than usual.

'Most men prefer to have more than one woman, but they usually don't want them to know about each other. I think you will have to find your own boyfriend,' Ada teased.

'I will not!' Rayn said, loud enough for anyone in the room to hear.

'All right, all right,' Ada said, motioning with her hands to suggest that Rayn should stop speaking so loudly. 'I said I will find a way, and I will. Trust me.'

Rayn lowered her eyes to the small table between them and whispered, 'I want to live with you.'

A long, awkward silence followed as Ada tried to figure out how to respond to her friend's admission.

Ada realised there was more to it than the practical question of future living arrangements. This was an expression of love. The pitiful, unreciprocated kind of love.

Shame washed over Ada as she saw the nature of their relationship for what it was. To Ada, theirs was a friendship of convenience. She had turned to Rayn when there was nobody else, and left her for months when she was back on her feet.

Ada had never questioned Rayn's commitment, or why she always accepted her ungrateful and illogical behaviour. It never occurred to her that Rayn might have feelings for her.

Cowardly, Ada moved on to a different subject.

'We have to get back to Sandcastle first. Unless we have something nasty chasing us again, I don't feel like running back. So we will probably spend two full days on the road, or even longer off it. The nights are cold, and men or beasts might attack us if we're seen.'

Rayn didn't reply or even look at her.

As was her way of handling emotional discomfort, Ada kept talking.

'But first, we have to survive until the morning. We have clothes and food, but we can't afford a room for the night. And we're already in the company of some mean-looking people.'

With still no reply forthcoming, Ada spent some time confirming her latter statement. The Mangled Miner was not the most appealing of inns, but it served the least expensive food. The drinking hall attracted clients who could not afford a visit to the finer establishments in town and those who were not welcome anywhere else. Dwarves and cripples. Dirty travellers, standing in small pools of mud that formed around their feet as they emptied their flagons. A battle-scarred giant of a man carried an unsightly whore over his shoulder as he headed for the rooms upstairs.

Then there were those whose reasons for preferring this particular location was less obvious. Those were the most interesting. Unable to learn their secrets and disadvantages from looking at them, Ada reached out with her spirit. Her vision blurred, and she closed her eyes to eliminate the distraction. As the shard underneath her tunic started emanating warmth, she grasped it with her hand. They were one.

She found Rayn, her spirit pure and timid. There were dwarves, their souls robust and unrevealing, like stone. She found the weak wills of drunkards and whoremongers, and she could listen to their unguarded thoughts as clearly as if they had spoken out loud. Spurred on by the rush of power, Ada drifted into the dark corners. She sensed a man, almost unconscious by hard drinking, desperately trying to silence the screams inside his head. A woman's screams. His woman? The smell of blood. The taste.

The man stirred, and Ada withdrew.

She drifted for some time as if floating in a slow river. From somewhere, there was a call. A distant whisper carried by a warm wind. She grasped for it, but it slipped away like water through sand.

Then, something else caught her attention, something strong. Beckoning for her, daring her to approach. Ada was unafraid; this was her domain. Nobody could find her in this place. Her curiosity had no boundaries, and she effortlessly bridged the distance between them.

Ada was drawn to the radiating power like a moth to a flame. His spirit was the likeness of a vast, black pearl. She moved closer to him, eager to learn his secrets. Breaking through the opaque shell, she found no resistance.

And yet, she could not. She was repulsed. Or rather, deflected, as she slid away like a drop of water on the polished surface. Confused, she tried again, with more force. To no avail.

Something tugged at her. Ada ignored the distraction, as she made a third, futile attempt.

'Ada!'

'WHAT?' Ada yelled. When she opened her eyes, she found Rayn holding her arm and shaking it, a worried expression on her face.

'What happened? Where did you go?' Rayn asked.

'Not now,' Ada said, as she left the table.

In a dark corner, she found him: the rider from the night before. Even here, he wore the wide hood pulled over his head, covering his face in shadows. His red eyes met hers as soon as she turned the corner.

'You live,' he greeted her.

'I do,' Ada said and pulled a chair up to the small table.

'And you were not … *assailed* by predators?'

'Not recently. Not yet.'

The red eyes narrowed. 'You play dangerous games, girl.'

'You have no idea,' she said, leaning forward over the table. Her opponent was unfamiliar, but this was her kind of game. 'Remove the hood. I want to see your face.'

A long pause ensued, as he considered her request.

Ada gasped as he slowly pulled back his hood. He was no man. No human male that is. But certainly a male. The skin was black, unblemished. His pointed chin did not show a hint of beard. The prominent cheekbones and pointed ears gave him a regal appearance. His hair was short stubble, white or grey, probably shaved off one or two weeks earlier. 'You're a black elf!'

The dark figure laughed, short and bitter. 'Most elves would object strongly to that!'

'But you look …' Ada started.

'Yes, I *look* like an elf. As the moon *looks* like the sun. But we are very different.'

Ada fell silent, searching her memories for the answer. The scary stories children told each other at night. The cruellest and dangerous of all the denizens of the underworld.

'You are *drow*,' she whispered.

'I am.'

'When I was a child, my mother told me that the drow were evil creatures living underground, eager to capture and enslave any human child they found. She told me never to enter a cave or a dark cellar.'

'True, but unlikely.'

Ada shivered. With fear or excitement, she could not tell.

The drow smiled, a wicked, knowing grin.

'I'm Ada.' She reached out with her right arm towards the drow, palm up, as customary for a formal greeting in Sandcastle.

The drow sat motionless for a few beats, looking at her. Somewhat awkwardly, he accepted the greeting by clutching her hand with both of his, one below and one above.

'Zekatar,' he whispered, apparently reluctant to reveal his name to anyone else.

His grip was firm, his slender hands strong and calloused. The drow radiated power, confidence and arrogance. Superior to her in every way, superior to everyone, and he knew. Ada felt small, insignificant, defeated. She was losing at the game she knew so well.

The drow pulled the hood back over his head and rose from the chair. Leaving two bits on the table as payment for his meal, he left Ada without another word.

Ada remained at the table until she'd regained her breath and composure. Then, she picked up the two bits and returned to Rayn.

Chapter 24: Night

Hobble woke. In his dream, he had been juggling stones. Lots of stones. And he excelled. Still, the sleep had been fitful. He yawned, stretched and went to the window. It was past midnight, and the streets were quiet. Large drops of rain fell and made lazy tapping noises on the windowsill. Gilmir lay in his bed, sleeping with his back to the room. At least Hobble thought he was asleep. It was hard to tell. The slender elf did not make a sound. Hobble shifted his gaze towards the door.

They needed money. In a pouch, hanging from his neck, he had the stone from the dead man. He slid the string over his head and took the stone out. Dark and smooth. Possibly a powerful artefact, but Hobble did not feel anything while holding it. Disappointing, really. He was in possession of a magical item, and as far as he could tell, it was useless to him. Gilmir was probably right, that the shard fortified some magical abilities one already possessed. Since he had none, magnifying them would not help him much. Maybe he should sell it? The right person would no doubt pay good money. The quality of his stone was perhaps not that great. However, he knew about more stones. Perhaps better quality, doubtless of more worth. And also something he could use?

Hobble dressed in silence and picked up his staff by the bedside. He inched the door open and slid out as soon as he fit through the opening. Stepping out in the dimly lit hallway, he paused. He looked up and down the corridor. Closing his eyes, he listened. The *tap tap* of the rain on the roof and a rhythmic rumbling was all he heard. Apart from the room he was staying in with the elf, five other rooms were emanating from the corridor. Last night, three of them had been occupied. One of the remaining vacant rooms was down the hall to the right. Hobble stalked down the passage. The number '5' was painted on the wooden door. The rumbling was the sound of someone snoring. Like the noise of rocks falling on rocks. It had to be the dwarf.

The door was solid, and the lock appeared to be of acceptable quality for a tavern bedroom door. Hobble leaned his staff against the door frame and felt around the edges of the door. When he came around to the right side, he took out a little flask of oil and with a small rag, he worked the oil into the hinges. Then he inspected the frame and the lock. After finding everything to his satisfaction, he produced his tools and started picking the lock. After a few moments, he heard the expected *click*. The door was open. Hobble put his tools away and listened. For long moments, he stood utterly still, reaching out with his senses. The snoring dwarf kept tumbling stones.

Finally, Hobble put his hand on the handle. This was always the scariest part. He took a deep breath and pushed the handle down. While he pushed the door open inch by inch, he hoped the hinges would keep quiet. Suddenly something stung his hand. A yelp crossed his lips, and he withdrew. The snoring stopped. A small needle protruded from a spring-loaded arm in the door frame by the handle. A single drop of blood showed where his hand had been pricked.

Hobble rubbed at his hand. Thoughts racing through his mind. The needle could have been there to wake the dwarf, relying on the fact that the sting would cause the intruder to make a sound. Although it worked that way this time, Hobble held no illusions. There would only be one, real reason for a spring-loaded needle in the door frame. Poison.

Hobble smelled the wound. A faint smell of water and plants, almost like a swamp. He bent to take a closer look at the needle. His hand started to prickle. Hobble frowned, looking down on his hand. It was going numb. *Balls!*

He turned and started back towards the room he shared with Gilmir. The numbness spread. Both arms and feet felt weird now. *Troll balls!*

His breathing became laboured. His right foot buckled. He fell to one knee. The world was spinning. *Disease-ridden, foul-smelling troll balls covering your face and strangling you!*

As he came to his feet, his entire body seemed to shut down, and he fell forward. Unable to dampen the fall with his hands, he crashed to the floor face first.

Gloves. You incompetent excuse for a burglar—use gloves!

With those final thoughts, the world stopped being.

Chapter 25: Brute

'It's horrible,' Rayn said.

Ada and Rayn had just entered the room they had rented for the two bits Ada had pilfered from the drow's table downstairs. The stench from cheap wine competed with those of sweat, vomit and piss for domination over the vile aroma in the small room. The fumes from an oil lamp on the small table between the two beds was by far the least unpleasant of the smells that threatened to overwhelm them.

'You get what you pay for in life,' Ada said, not entirely convinced by her own logic.

'How can anyone sleep in this filth?' Rayn asked, pointing to the torn and stained linen on the beds.

'If you've had enough wine, you will sleep anywhere,' Ada said. 'Which will make things even worse for the next guest, of course.'

Rayn was temporarily distracted by a particularly high scream from one of the whores earning their bits in the nearby rooms. The thin walls did little to dampen the sounds of coarse laughter, squeaking beds and exaggerated groans. From the drinking hall below, they heard fighting and breaking of glass.

'How can anyone sleep with this noise?' Rayn said.

Despite their circumstances, Ada couldn't help smiling at her friend's questions. She answered in kind: 'If you've had enough wine, you will sleep anywhere!'

A series of knocks, groans and screams revealed that the girl next door would soon be looking for a new client. Rayn turned away, blushing.

Ada laughed. 'Most of them aren't trying to sleep yet.'

Rayn sat down on the bed, sobbing. 'I hate this place!'

Ada sat beside her and put her arm around her shoulders. 'I know, and I'm sorry you have to experience this. We'll leave for home at first light tomorrow. Just one more night here. It's a terrible place, but at least we're safe. Only fleas and lice can bother us tonight.'

Rayn soon stopped sobbing, her body gradually relaxing as she leaned against Ada. For the first time since Ada entered the apothecary in Sandcastle, there was nothing they had to do. Apart from sleep, or at least wait, until morning. Then they would be on their way. Compared to Sha'ton, Sandcastle was paradise.

Heavy steps in the hallway demanded their attention, as they stopped outside the door. After a few beats, there was a single knock on the door. There was no need for a second knock, as the first sent the door swinging inwards and slamming against the wall.

A huge figure filled the entire doorway. As he bowed to get his head under the frame, Ada recognised the ugly, scarred veteran she had seen carrying a woman up the stairs a few hours earlier. For a moment, he seemed confused until he fixed his gaze on Ada. In two steps, he stood before her, his excitement in plain sight. He grabbed her arm and lifted her from the bed.

'I've been looking for you,' he grunted and turned towards the empty bed. Keeping Ada's arm in a firm grip, he effortlessly held the slender woman above the floor and swung her around. With his free arm, he started groping her and tugging at her clothes.

'Hey! Get your filthy hands off me!' Ada yelled. She was no stranger to aggressive men, but this was worse than anyone she had experienced before.

The brute laughed. 'Yes, please yell and scream. I like that. You're going to cry soon, for real. I like that even more.'

Ada knew the truth of that. 'Go away! I'm not a whore!'

He laughed again, differently this time. 'Oh, yes, you are. I've already paid for you. All of two bits!'

His words stunned Ada. *Two bits?* She hung limp, as the implications of that possibility raced through her mind. *The drow? Surely not? Or would he?*

'Leave her alone!' Rayn shouted and banged her fists against the giant's back.

Without turning to face her, the veteran sent Rayn sprawling with a forceful backhand strike to her face. The impact sent the half-elf flying over the bed, slamming her head against the wall.

'Rayn!' Ada cried, twisting her upper body in a futile attempt to see past the man blocking her view.

'You're a pretty one,' the brute said, his free arm pinching and squeezing her with increasing intensity.

He's going to kill me, one way or the other. The realisation focused her mind. She went limp, allowing him to grope her and pull down her pants. Ignoring the repulsion, she felt the heat grow with her, fuelled by fear and desperation. A warm wind brushed against her face, reassuring her. Providing strength and resolve.

With a sudden movement, Ada kicked the table between the beds, causing the lamp to land at the bed they had been sitting on. The oil spilt and caught fire among the straw and linen. In beats, flames climbed up the wooden wall.

The veteran hesitated as if he was trying to figure whether this bothersome fire would prevent him from having his way with the girl.

Ada settled the issue. The fear was gone, replaced by an absolute determination. Her entire body was filled with heat, a hundred times hotter and a thousand times more pleasant than a warm bath. The surge of power was intoxicating, more than any drug or any feeling she'd ever known.

She calmly looked into his eyes as she channelled the essence of fire. Ada became fire. As easily as exhaling, she released the fire within her, consuming the brute's torso and face in heartbeats.

There was a voice in the warm wind. Ada perceived it was pleased with her, though she could not discern the whispering words before it disappeared.

As the power drained from her body, the fire in the room intensified. Ada noticed Rayn sprawled on the floor, dangerously close to the burning bed. She quickly pulled her pants back on and dragged Rayn out of the room.

Chapter 26: Debt

Gilmir woke with a start. Rubbing his nailless finger, he tried to distinguish dream from reality. Had there been a sound from the hallway? He sat up. His body was aching as usual but less than in a long time. The bed Hobble used was empty. It was dark outside, the hour was sometime between midnight and first light. He heard a small scratching noise from the corridor outside the room. He dressed, and picked up the knife Hobble had given him. Holding it in his right hand but concealed behind his wrist. Hearing footsteps outside, he opened the door with his left hand and peaked out. Hobble lay face down in the corridor a few steps from the door. Behind him stood Tracks looking down on Hobble's staff, which he held in his hands.

'What's going on?' Gilmir asked.

Tracks looked up, as he only now realised that Gilmir had stepped out in the hallway. 'This little rat broke into my room.'

Despite his words, the dwarf did not seem overly aggressive. Gilmir took a few steps forward, sitting down by the halfling. There was no mark on the back of his head—no indication that Tracks had hit him with the staff. Turning him over, the body was limp but stiff as if he had been dead for hours. Which, of course, could not be the case. His face was bloody, probably from a broken nose. Gilmir looked up at Tracks.

'What's wrong with him?'

'Dead.'

'No. He is not. Not yet. Did you poison him?'

'I didn't do a thing. He broke into my room. He got himself poisoned.'

Gilmir lifted the halfling's hands. He found a tiny pinprick of a wound. Feeling the skin around, he shook his head. He gathered a drop of blood on his fingertip and held it to his nose. Then he stuck his tongue to it.

'Luin quácë,' he muttered, shaking his head again.

'Dead.' Tracks insisted.

'He soon will be. You poisoned him with the poison from the skin of the blue frog—Luin quácë,'

Tracks shrugged. 'I didn't do any—'

'Give me the antidote,' Gilmir said, cutting the dwarf short.

Tracks stood staring at the elf. Gilmir rose.

'Look, I understand you didn't do anything other than guarding your door with a clever trap. However, I know there is an antidote to the blue frog poison and I know you have it. You can't predict who will try to enter your room, and you would be a fool not to have an antidote in the case of a misunderstanding. My friend here is dead soon, and then it will be too late. We could never reverse that. On the other hand, if you give me the antidote, you can always kill him later. All options are still open.'

'As you know, tall one, the poison is expensive. The cure even more so. I see no reason wasting the antidote on a common thief.'

'We would owe you.'

The dwarf stared at him. Gilmir glanced down at halfling at his feet. The little body drew breath. The breaths had become shallow and further between. Meeting Tracks eyes again he spoke in his most persuasive tone:

'We will make it worth your while.'

'Pfft, I will probably regret this,' Tracks said, throwing a vial to Gilmir. 'We will speak tomorrow, elf.' He put the staff against the wall and turned, walking to his room.

Gilmir wasted no time. He lifted Hobble up in a sitting position and emptied the vial down his throat. Hoping it was not too late.

Chapter 27: Plan

The halfling stirred and mumbled something about silver. It was afternoon and Hobble had been sleeping since Gilmir gave him the antidote. Gilmir had carried him to his bed and spent the rest of the time waiting. Sometime during the night, a fire broke out in the city. The sky turned red with flickering light, and people had been shouting about fire and witches. Apart from that, the night passed in silence. Hobble's broken nose made wheezing noises with every breath, but other than that, he slept peacefully. Gilmir was not sure what to expect in terms of after-effects of the poison, but Hobble should be fine if he had received the cure in time. That, however, was a big *if*. Gilmir knew of people who ended up as drooling idiots after similar ordeals.

'Gloves!' Hobble said, sitting up. He looked around the small room before his hands went to his face. 'Aouu!' He touched his nose with his fingers as if checking to see if it was still attached. 'Disease-ridden, foul-smelling, troll balls!'

Gilmir analysed the scene in front of him. The halfling examined his broken nose. That was good. Normal. His speech was incongruent. The words were real but had no bearing on the situation. The last sentence-like statement could be some sort of curse. He had not heard the halfling utter similar before, but if the little people swore by uttering different names for genitals like humans did, it might be swearing. Probably was. Either way, Gilmir needed more proof of Hobble's sanity.

'What is the last thing you remember, Hobble?'

Hobble glanced at him but did not answer. He still held his nose.

'Last night, you went out of this room, and then what? What happened?' Gilmir prodded.

'I don't remember,' Hobble said in a nasal voice.

Amnesia. Not a good sign.

'You don't remember, or are you too embarrassed to talk about it? Tell me the truth, it is important.'

Hobble stared at him once more, before he lay back on his bed again. 'My nose hurt, and my body aches all over. Leave me alone!'

'Sure. You can deal with the mad dwarf in Room 5 by yourself.'

Hobble sat up. 'Wait, what? What happened?'

'You first. What did you do after leaving this room last night?'

'Fine! We needed money. I went to Tracks's room. He had a needle trap, I did not wear gloves.'

'What were you going to steal?'

'I don't know! Something valuable. We need money, remember?'

Gilmir was reassured and worried at the same time. The halfling appeared rational, or at least it did not seem like the poison had damaged his mental capacities. However, there were other concerns.

'Are you usually this stupid?' It was not an insult, it was a genuine concern.

'Piss off!'

Gilmir took a deep breath. 'Either way, we have to meet Tracks today. To explain how we are supposed to repay him.'

'Repay him for what?' Hobble asked. 'I didn't steal anything.'

'For saving your life.'

'SAVING my life?!'

'Yeah, you were dying. He had an antidote. You could say he held all the cards. I had nothing to offer. I said we would make it worth his while.' Gilmir shrugged and spread his hands in an apologetic gesture. 'However, I have no idea how we're supposed to do that.'

Hobble sat back up, the emotions fading from his face and body. 'Can't you just get rid of him?'

This time, Gilmir stared. 'Why do you say that?'

'I don't know. I thought … You seem to …' Hobble went silent for a moment. 'It seems to solve a lot of our problems.'

'And add a ton of new ones. No, think of something else.'

The halfling pursed his lips and nodded slowly. The room went silent once again.

'What's that?' Hobble said, looking towards the window.

Gilmir turned in his chair. Outside, small flakes of grey and white drifted passed the window. 'There was a fire.'

'Aha.'

'Let me see that stone of yours,' Gilmir said.

'No!' Hobble seemed surprised by his own ferocity. 'I meant, why?'

'Maybe we should start by selling it,' Gilmir said studying the halfling.

Hobble produced the stone from a pouch inside his tunic. Handing it over, he said, 'Yeah, maybe. I have been thinking the same.'

Gilmir examined the stone once more. He closed his eyes and reached out with all his senses. First, he noticed the static between his own stone and Hobbles' black shard. This he ignored, closing in on the black stone. The energy was apparent but not very strong, clearly inferior to his purple shard. However, there was a clear energy, like a pulsating light. And something else. Something within the light. A shadow? A taint? He could not say, but it felt like somebody, or something influenced it in some way. Gilmir withdrew.

'I know you wanted a shard for yourself, but I am not sure this is good for you. Have you felt anything? Has it helped you in some way?'

'No, I don't think so. But then, I haven't had it for that long. Maybe it takes time.'

'Maybe. However, I don't like the feel of this one.' Gilmir handed it over. 'I think it is tainted somehow.'

'Maybe it is the interaction with the other, the one you have? Didn't you say that having two would cause trouble?'

'No, it's not that, it's something else. Something to do with the dead man who carried it or the one who put it there. I don't know, but I don't like it. And you've had no training. If we can sell it —I think it would be a double blessing.'

'Okay. I am down with that,' Hobble said, putting the stone back in the pouch.

'Good. I have an idea. I will start looking into finding a buyer. In the meantime, can you find an alternative way to get some money? The arena scheme or something else. It's better if we have some alternatives.'

'Sure,' Hobble said, nodding.

Gilmir tilted his head, listening. 'He is coming. Tracks is coming.'

Soon footsteps sounded from the hallway. A moment later, there was a loud knock on the door. The elf and the halfling drew a simultaneous breath and glanced at each other.

Chapter 28: Sentence

'Mnnghhh,' Ada said.

It was not what she intended to say, but the rag in her mouth complicated things. The tight blindfold over her eyes similarly complicated the use of her eyes.

Murder they had said. And arson. Someone in the background had mumbled 'witchcraft' and 'sorcery' as well, pointing out that no normal fire would cause the damage found on what remained of the veteran's body. The acting judge dismissed the notion, explaining there were no laws against witchcraft in Shacktown and that the two women would be sentenced to death regardless of how or why they started the fire, destroying four buildings and killing three people.

Ada and Rayn had not been allowed to explain or defend themselves. They were apprehended by armed men as soon as they exited the burning inn. Their hands tied behind their backs, and they were gagged before someone pulled a sack over their heads. Later, they were dumped on the floor in a cold dungeon cell, and chained to the wall.

There had been no trial. Hours or days ago, Ada couldn't tell, some men entered their cell. They briefly discussed the case and the charges among themselves, until one of them concluded and sentenced them to death. Some others uttered their approval, and the company left. The cell door slammed shut and had not been opened since.

Before the mock trial, they'd been given brief opportunities to eat and drink. Two guards carrying torches replaced the sacks over their heads with blindfolds. For two beats, Ada had been able to see with eyes half-blinded by the torchlight. She confirmed what she already had perceived with her other senses: she was in a small dungeon cell, and Rayn was in the opposite corner, just outside her reach.

After the blindfolds were in place, the gag was removed and replaced with a chunk of old bread. Ada chewed as fast as possible, but her mouth was still half full of bread when the guard forced the tip of a wineskin between her lips. The sour wine dissolved the bread, and she swallowed the unsavoury meal. When she opened her mouth to draw a breath of air, the guards quickly replaced the gag.

Five times before the trial, the feeding ritual had been repeated, but not after. They were sentenced to death, but nobody had mentioned how they were to be killed. Ada grew increasingly aware that there was no need for an execution if they did not get anything to drink.

Her biggest concern, however, was that she did not hear anything from Rayn. She was also gagged, of course. But until recently Ada could hear her breathing, shuffling her feet or the occasional muffled yelp when a rat got too curious. Now, there was nothing. The half-elf had been conscious when they escaped the fire, but they were seized before Ada could examine her wounds. She had slammed her head against the wall when the brute hit her, and most likely suffered burn injuries.

In their eagerness to prevent the two arsenious witches causing any more damage, the mob had pulled sacks over their heads and carried them to the dungeons. Thus, nobody found the stone Ada kept in a pouch attached to a leather string around her neck. Rayn would probably still have hers, too.

The power that enabled her to incinerate a man days before felt so faint and distant in the cold dungeon. She was weakened from the exposure, hunger and thirst, and there was no source of heat or other elements to draw from.

Boosted by her starfall shard, Ada went beyond the limits of her own being to search for her friend. Typically, the presence of rodents would be mere distractions, the mindless chatter from their weak spirits easily ignored or overlooked, like tiny stars in comparison to the moon. But Rayn's soul was so fragile—hardly noticeable among half a dozen rats. Ada found her, pale and faded. Her life essence almost extinguished. She was alive but not for long.

Fearing for her friend's life, Ada intensified her efforts. Removing the barriers separating her from the outside world, she drew on the power of the shards to unite with Rayn's spirit. The noise from the rats multiplied, and the distant echoes of hundreds of thoughts and voices filled her mind. The stone around her neck started vibrating, creating a high-pitched tone.

'Rayn, I'm here. Wake up.'

There was no reply.

In desperation, Ada pushed even further, ignoring the incessant noise from nearby people and animals. A warm wind embraced her naked spirit. There was a whisper, and even though she could not understand the words, it comforted and encouraged her.

The half-elf was too weak to resist as Ada trespassed the boundaries that separated them. They merged, allowing Ada to sense with Rayn's senses and experience her emotions.

Ada's first clue was the absence of thoughts. If Rayn was awake, she did not think. If she was sleeping, she was not dreaming. A growing premonition drove her further, connecting with her friend's senses. Ada stirred as she sensed the pain. The incessant, sharp, ever-present sting from the burnt skin on her right thigh and hip. And the regular thuds, the waves of numbing pain that washed through her head with every weak heartbeat.

Unable to do anything for Rayn, Ada stayed with her. Sensing the fear and pain subsiding, replaced by exhaustion and sorrow as the body slowly capitulated. Her inhalations were weaker and further between, to the point where she did not breathe at all. But every time, she would inhale sharply, and the breathing pattern improved. Devoid of light, hourglasses or any other ways to measure the passing of time, Ada started counting those forceful inhalations that followed a prolonged pause. For the first hundred or so cycles, she waited expectantly for Rayn to inhale, and felt relief when it happened.

But then, gradually, Ada found herself hoping that the innerving breathing would stop, that Rayn would remain quiet.

'Please, just die,' Ada whispered.

In the darkness a few feet away, Rayn inhaled forcefully. For the four hundred and thirtieth time since Ada started counting.

'Yes, you're right,' Ada said. 'I'm terrible.'

Ada was no stranger to feeling shame, but this was worse than anything she had experienced before. Far worse than anything she had ever done before.

Her stomach twisted into a firm knot, and her body curled up as she tried to vomit. She rolled sideways, felt the acid burn in her throat, and the foul taste filled her mouth as she half coughed, half spat a tiny amount of slime.

She coughed again, and leaned back against the cold stone wall, allowing herself to fully submerge in the bittersweet pool of equal parts self-pity and self-loathing.

'You were the only decent person in my life. The only person to love me. And I took advantage of you, as I've done before. I burned down your home, and dragged you to this horrible place. You gave your life to protect me, and all I can do is to suggest you die faster.'

Ada stopped counting, and surrendered to the hopelessness. Eventually, Rayn's breathing rhythms changed, becoming more laborious and irregular. Hers was no quiet passing, no peaceful sleep. For hours, Rayn fought a losing battle, until she did not possess the strength to draw one more breath. As her spirit departed, the power of her starglass shard extinguished like a candle.

Ada was alone in the dark.

Chapter 29: Foul

'It used to be easier killing rats,' Tracks said, pulling out a chair on the other side of the table from where Gilmir sat. The dwarf did not look at Hobble who still sat on the bed, legs crossed, back to the wall. 'What deal you have for me, elf?'

'I haven't been in this city for long, but it strikes me as the sort of place where one would need all the friends one could get.'

'You better have something else, tall one. I have little use for friends, and less of thieving, rat friends.'

Gilmir held up a hand. 'I understand. Let us trade,' he said, well aware that dwarves were not fast to make friends, but appreciated a proper trade arrangement. 'We have a shard from the starfall. You can get it for a decent price. An excellent price.'

'Let's see it.'

Hobble gave Gilmir a glance but handed over the dark stone. The dwarf accepted, lifted it to the light from the window and peered at it. His mouth started to move, but Gilmir could not discern any words. Tracks folded his rough hands over the stone, and his eyes seemed to unfocus, before they rolled up into his head, so that only white showed. Gilmir glanced at Hobble, but the halfling only shrugged. For long moments, they sat like that.

'Nah, I don't want this.' Tracks opened his eyes, and handed the shard to Gilmir.

'Why?' Gilmir asked.

'That stone … it's not a good stone.'

'What is wrong with it?'

'It is foul.'

Gilmir studied the dwarf hoping for an explanation. After a few moments, the dwarf spoke.

'Where did you find it?'

Gilmir considered the question. He did not trust the volatile dwarf. However, nor did he see how revealing information about the stone would be a problem. Besides, giving some insights on the shard could help them get in Tracks's good grace. 'It was inside a walking corpse.'

'Necromancy!' Tracks spat on the floor.

The room went silent again. Gilmir glanced at Hobble, unsure how to proceed. The dwarf spoke first.

'I hope you have something else for me, elf.'

Gilmir spread his hands. 'Not at the moment, master dwarf. We need to sell that shard first.'

Tracks grunted. 'Do you even know where to start?'

'We know some of Voan's men are looking for one.'

'Voan? THE Voan?'

'I didn't realise there was more than one,' Gilmir said.

'Voan is a dangerous man. You know he is one of the councilmen?'

'Councilmen?' Hobble said.

Still looking at Gilmir, Tracks said, 'Shacktown is run by five councilmen. Voan is one of them. The council calls all the shots round here, and the five are considered the most dangerous people in this most dangerous of towns.'

'I thought the baron ruled the city?' Hobble said.

'He is a puppet,' Tracks said.

'Do you know him? Voan, I mean?' Gilmir said.

'I've traded with him before, but I don't any more.'

'Why?'

'I don't trust him. And want nothing to do with him.'

'I see.'

'So, you keep me out of it. Understand?' This time the dwarf looked at both of them.

Gilmir nodded.

Pushing back the chair, the dwarf got to his feet. He turned towards the door, but stopped halfway, staring at Hobble. 'I'll let you live, for now, rat. But you better prove yourself useful in the coming days. I have not forgotten nor forgiven.'

Chapter 30: Chris

Later that evening Gilmir went down to the inn's common room. He had persuaded Hobble to give him coins for a glass of wine. Finding a place in the back corner, he sat down. He located the serving girl called Chris and lifted a finger when they made eye contact. Putting the coins on the table, he ordered a glass of wine.

When Chris returned with his drink, Gilmir said, 'I wondered if you could help me with something?'

'Sorry, it's busy tonight. I have no time to chat,' Chris said with a slight rural dialect. She picked up the coins and turned with practised efficiency.

'I am sorry about your father.'

Chris stopped, and turned. Staring at him with narrowed eyes, she asked, 'What do you know about my father?'

'I'll tell you, if you help me with something.'

Chris studied him for a moment, as if she was seeing him for the first time. Gilmir knew he would get the help he needed.

'I'll come back when I have a break,' the serving girl said, before heading back towards the bar. A brown armless dress revealed the girl's arms. The right limb visibly more muscular than the left. Gilmir let his glance fall to her legs. The left more toned than the right. Another piece of the puzzle.

A half hour later Chris came and took a seat on the other side of the table. The glass in front of Gilmir was almost empty despite his attempts to make the wine last. Fortunately, in that regard, the wine was not especially tasty. It was a dull, fruity thing, with a stale, earthy aftertaste. However, it was wine.

'Any chance of a refill?' Gilmir asked, lifting the glass and shaking it.

'If you have the coin,' Chris said without a smile.

Gilmir sighed and put the glass back down.

'What do you know about my father?' Chris asked.

'You first. Do you know an old drunkard called Saendar? I need to speak to him. Can you arrange a meeting?'

'I know of him, yes, everybody does,' Chris said, frowning. 'But …' She trailed off, her gaze locked on his. 'Okay, that is all? A meeting with Saendar? When?'

'Sometime tomorrow is fine.'

'Okay, I'll make it happen. Now, tell me what you know about my father.'

Gilmir realised he should not say anything until after the meeting. There was no possible way to tell how she would react to what he had to say. In fact, he did not have much, and she would most likely end up disappointed. He could ruin it all by telling her now. On the other hand, he did not remember the last time he spoke to a female. It felt good. Normal. Even a human girl. He took the last sip of wine, and held up the empty glass.

'Fine!' Chris took the glass and stomped off.

This is going great, Gilmir thought, chuckling to himself.

Soon Chris thumped the wine glass on the table in front of Gilmir. 'Now, sir, you start speaking.'

'Of course, fair lady,' Gilmir said, lifting the glass. 'We have a deal. I tell you what I know of your father, and you set up the meeting with Saendar tomorrow?'

'Yes, spill it!'

Gilmir took a sip of the wine to hide his smile. He enjoyed this more than he should. Putting down the glass, he started his tale.

'You and your father lived in the countryside. Just the two of you.' Gilmir studied the girl intently while he spoke the last sentence, watching her reaction. Her eyes widened a little, her pupils dilated ever so slightly. 'He used to be a soldier.' Chris leaned forward a little. Another hit. 'When he died, you moved into the city.' No reaction. 'You got a job here. The owner is an old friend of your old man?' The girl's eyebrows knitted. *Falling stars, he was slipping.* 'Your father taught you everything you know, you were very close.' A hint of something in her eyes. A little generic, but closer to the target. Chris lent back on her chair and crossed her arms. She was on to him. He leapt for it. 'His name was Christopher. He was a sergeant in the Grey Kings army until he retired. You still have his sword.' Her eyes shifted to the left, the pupils growing a bit again. *A strong finish,* Gilmir congratulated himself. Lifting the glass to his lips, he took another sip of wine. It was getting better.

'You did not know my father, so how did you come up with that story?'

Gilmir studied the girl for a moment. Either he had missed more on his deduction than he thought or there was more to this young human woman than he had first suspected.

Gilmir cleared his throat. 'The bracelet you are wearing, and the belt you wore the other day— they are both more fitting to a grown man. The belt is similar to the weapons belts used in the army, and worn. Especially where one would expect a scabbard to be fastened. I suspect the bracelet is of sentimental value. Whereas the belt serves several purposes. Your dialect revealed that you've not grown up in the city, although you try to hide it. And "Chris?" Gender-neutral names are not common for humans living in the countryside. I guess you took your father's name or a short version when you moved here. After he died, that is. Your hand is calloused'—Gilmir nodded towards her hands now resting in the girl's lap—'indicating that you are used to harder work than serving drinks.'

Chris stared at him in silence for a while. Crossing her arms again, she said, 'And the part of him being a sergeant in the Grey Kings army?'

'Mostly a guess,' Gilmir said, studying her.

'So you did in fact not know him.' Chris could not hide her disappointment, moisture gathering in her eyes.

A stab of bad conscience hit Gilmir who opened his mouth to reply. But the girl was faster.

'Or maybe,' Chris said, balling her fists, 'I stole the stuff from an *old*, annoying guy, after beating him to death with my bare hands for telling me nonsense stories about my life!' The young woman pushed her chair back, and rose.

'Wait. If you do set up the meeting with Saendar, I can give you some pointers on your swordplay.' Chris stood staring down at him. 'For a small fee, of course,' Gilmir added with a smile.

'How do you … What do *you* know about swordplay?!'

'I know enough to tell that your stance is unbalanced. You always lead with your rapier, and trail with your left foot. Which is fine for fencing at your uncle's garden party, but not effective in real combat. When that *old* man comes at you with murder in his eyes, you need more balance. Both in your body and in your stance.' He did not like that the girl had indicated that he was old. For an elf, he was young. Besides, he was not supposed to show any signs of ageing. The time in the prison cell had taken its toll, and, although feeling much better, he still had a lot of mending to do.

'I'll set up the meeting.' Chris turned on her heels.

Chapter 31: Spirits

In the darkness, Ada reached out. She passed effortlessly through the stone and mortar barriers that kept her body imprisoned in the dungeon cell.

A prison guard stirred as Ada nudged him tentatively. His spirit radiated fear and anger, like that of an animal trying to survive in a hostile environment. Unable to discern the source of the distraction, he rose.

'I think I heard something down the hall,' he said. His voice sounded like a sword scraped over stone.

Ada remained impassive, as she considered the effects of the greatly improved presence spell, enhanced by the starglass resting against her chest. This was the first time she had been able to eavesdrop on people by use of her magic. Would they be able to hear her if she moved or spoke?

This was not the time to find out.

Ada drifted further, leaving behind the plagued denizens of the dungeon. As she approached ground level, she sensed hundreds of souls nearby, most of them sleeping.

She found herself in an inn, an hour or two before dawn. A man was working in the kitchen, and a woman was using the chamber pot in one of the rooms upstairs.

Ada ignored the commoners, her attention drawn to the tortured spirit above, screaming wordlessly into the night.

His soul was noble and scarred like a burnt stallion. Even in his sleep, the elven spirit burned brighter than any other. Red fires, fuelled by anger, or pain.

Ada knew this one.

'Gilmir,' she whispered.

Ada heard her own voice, somewhere. Whether down in the dungeon cell, in the inn above or in some parallel, spiritual dimension, she could not tell. She tried again, raising her voice to a normal, conversational level.

'Gilmir.'

There was no response. The elf spirit writhed. A dream, or a nightmare.

'Gilmir!' Ada shouted. Or at least, she thought she did.

The elf couldn't hear her. Or, if he heard, it was not enough to pull him out of his dream.

Chapter 32: Dream

In his dream, Gilmir was back in the dungeon. He lay on his back on the stone table. A rag smelling of sweat and human anxiety was tied around his head, covering his eyes. He smelled blood and metal, and something else. An animal scent. No, reptile. Footsteps approached. He sensed someone lean over him. The torturer's breath came rapid and shallow, smelling of lavender and pipe weed. Fánë alma—the elven tobacco made mostly of white flower petals. Gilmir pushed the strange notion that his torturer smoked elven tobacco to the back of his mind, and concentrated on his breathing. Slow and steady. The pain was not getting any worse. That was his consolation. He had been drowned, burned and cut, but still, the torturer was not satisfied.

A cold hand grasped his and pressed down on the hard stone. Metal pressed against the tip of his index finger.

'You will break,' said the coarse voice near his ear. 'It's better for you to tell me sooner rather than later. For in the end, you will talk, you will tell me what I want to know.'

The metal pressed harder against his fingertip. A tong, Gilmir realised. It clamped down on the tip of his fingernail. The pressure decreased before the tong was pushed further in on the nail and then clasped down again. In the background, Magnus the prison guard laughed. The one who always followed him to the torture chamber. And relished in other people's pain.

'It's your own fault, you know,' the torturer whispered, 'Never lie helpless on the table of a torturer!'

Gilmir hardly registered the words. He fought a battle inside his head. In his mind, he screamed. In his mind, he cried. He talked. He told everything the man wanted to know. His heart hammered in his throat. A taste of metal flowed over his tongue. Water started to gather in his mouth. A sure sign that he was about to vomit. This was the worst part. The part where he knew what was coming and could do nothing but wait. He focused his mind. Retook control of his breathing. He would not lose this battle.

'I feel sorry for you if you think this matters to me,' Gilmir said with the most disinterested voice his training allowed him to produce. 'If you think that an amateur like yourself can hurt me in any way that even resembles what awaits me if I come back after telling you something. Anything. You are a sorry excuse for a man. Even worse, you are a sorry excuse for a torturer. You have no technique, no finesse, no strategy. You're just evil and perverted. But worse than that, you are not any good at it. In short …'

The tong started to pull on his nail, and the torturer used the distraction to start the questions again. 'Who sent you?'

'I am from the fourth island on the fifth ocean,' Gilmir said.

'What are you doing here?'

'I came here to make a commotion.'

'You will regret this, elf!' The torturer pulled harder on the tong holding his nail. 'WHAT ARE YOU DOING HERE?'

'I came with seven songs to sing.'

'Who are you?'

'I am the second son of the third king,' Gilmir said through gritted teeth, gasping between each word.

'Your choice, elf.'

Gilmir lost control. Gave in. The words came spilling out of his mouth.

> I am the second son of the third king,
>
> from the fourth island on the fifth ocean,
>
> from the sixth road, not on the wing,
>
> I came here to make a commotion,
>
> I came with seven songs to sing.

He recited the old children's verse. Over and over. Until the pain stopped.

Chapter 33: Bits Arena

While Hobble limped to the arena the next morning, he pondered the plan Gilmir had presented. It was a good scheme. All he had to do on this day was to go to the arena and lose a few fights. Until now, he had won most, but barely. He could have won all of them easy enough. But this was the arena where the consequences for the loser was, for the most part, harmless. There is only one rule in Bits Arena. You are not allowed to kill or severely injury your opponent. The punishment, like for most crimes in the town, is to fight in the stadium, the greatest arena in Sha'ton.

There are several reasons a spot in the stadium is considered a punishment.

First and foremost, there is no rule against killing or maiming in the stadium.

The second reason is that if you're usually fighting in the Bits Arena, you're severely under-qualified for a contest in the stadium. If you are lucky, you end up in the first bouts. Those fights are meant to warm up the crowd, and most of your opponents are just as incompetent as you are. If you happen to survive, you can look forward to more of the same the following weekend.

If you are *not* lucky, you spend your final moments mauled or lacerated by some exotic beast or monster from the underworld. The purpose of such a demonstration of destructive talents is, of course, to make sure the rich ladies in the stands know how fierce these beasts are when the real fighters—the gladiators—face them.

Finally, as a criminal you will receive no reward from the stadium, except for your freedom when the sentence is served. Few criminals ever made it out of the stadium alive.

Approaching the arena, Hobble moved slower and leaned heavier on the staff. He hobbled over to Faster, short for fight master. Faster was a burly man with a balding head and stubbly beard. Three teenagers were waiting in line to sign up for fights. When Hobble reached the end of the line, Faster made his typical joke.

'Next!' he said, lifting his hand to shield the sun while he surveyed the surrounding area, pointedly looking over Hobbles head. 'No one else, okay, then!'

Hobble cleared his throat.

'Oh, sorry, didn't see you down there, cripple,' Faster said, while the youngsters around them chuckled nervously.

'Set me up for three fights this morning, master Faster,' Hobble said, addressing Faster in the polite, but ridiculous, way he always did.

'I do like to be called "master" fight master,' the burly man said chuckling, 'but tell me, cripple, do you get off by the beating you receive or are you paying off some debt? Yes, of course, you are! You have to pay those whores double don't you, as they can't feel when they are getting shagged.' Faster wiggled his little finger in front of Hobble.

'That makes no sense,' Hobble muttered under his breath. The pain from his broken nose made it difficult to tolerate the customary insults.

'What's that?' Faster cupped a hand behind his ear, 'I can't hear you down there.'

'Do I get my three fights?'

'Yeah, yeah, I wouldn't stand between a man and his whore, even a half-man. Watch the board for your matches. And have someone lift you up if you can't see it, I won't tolerate any hold-ups in my arena.'

Hobble waited for Faster to scribble down the last contenders, and match them in pairs on the stone board. Already in the third match, he would get his first chance to lose. Faster scratched "CRIPLE" and "TOMI" on the two columns in the third row. Tomi, or Tommy, as folks who could actually spell would name him, was a farmer's boy with big ears. In fact, Hobble would not mind losing against him. He was a decent sort and had moved to the city after his father died last winter. Hobble spotted the oversized boy in the crowd and gave him a nod. Tommy nodded back with a slight smile and a shrug of his round shoulders. Turning back to the arena, Hobble saw two youths stepping into the ring.

'Knuckles or sticks?' Faster asked.

In Bits Arena, the fights were either barehanded or with wooden weapons. In a heap nearby, one could find all sorts of sticks, clubs and staves. Most fighters brought their own clubs or other weapons of choice. The fighter in the first column got to choose how the match was fought.

'Sticks,' the boy said, lifting two clubs to emphasise his choice.

The other boy lifted his club to show that he was ready.

'No killing, no murder, no slaying nor slaughter!' Faster cried out raising his arms. Swinging his arm downward, he shouted, 'Fight!'

Hobble turned away from the fight and glanced around. He needed to piss. Shaking his head, he made for an alley; this always happened before a fight.

When he came back, the first fight was over. Also, the second match went fast and soon Hobble stood ready in the ring of stones. A commotion made Hobble turn his head. A tall man stood in front of Faster, talking. The fight master seemed less than happy, but in the end, he nodded. Faster stepped into the ring and cleared his throat.

'Tommy has forfeited. Luckily this gentleman has agreed to take young Tommy's place, so that we can keep the schedule.' Faster indicated the tall man with his arm. A sigh went through the crowd. 'Next fight will be Cripple against Victor,' Faster continued. 'Knuckles or sticks?'

Victor was tall and muscular. He appeared more like a bouncer than a typical Bits Arena fighter. Stepping into the ring with one arm raised, he let his eyes glide over the crowd with a grin on his square face. Hobble realised that losing this match would not be difficult. But more than that, he realised he was in trouble. This could not be a coincidence. He had seen Tommy less than a quartermark ago, seemingly in good spirits and ready to fight. Something was out of order, and he was the intended target. Precisely what he was the target for, he did not know. But, he was convinced that the one rule of Bits Arena would be considered a vague recommendation in the upcoming fight. Hobble tightened his grip on the staff and answered. 'Sticks.'

Victor smiled and stepped over to the pile of wooden weapons. After picking up two clubs, he returned to the ring. Faster nodded and went into his routine.

'No killing, no murder, no slaying nor slaughter!' Faster said, raising his arms. 'Fight!'

Hobble held the staff in front of him, horizontal, with both hands. Victor came forward, left stick in front of him, the right held high beside his head. Circling, Hobble tried to gauge his opponent, but Victor wasted no time. Leading with his left stick, he made three fast attacks, like a boxer's jabs. However, he was not aiming for Hobble's head or body, he targeted the hands holding the staff. Hobble had to move the staff sideways to avoid getting his hands cracked. When the right club came chopping down, Hobble had to jump back to avoid the blow. It took all his skill to land without falling or revealing that his club foot was not a hindrance after all. He limped more pronounced for a few steps, wincing all the while.

Victor came on, smiling. Hobble considered letting the man hit him sooner rather than later. Let the jabs connect, lose the staff and concede defeat. However, something in the man's eyes made him doubt that he would get off that easy. He had to be careful. This man was not here to earn a few bits knocking kids and cripples around. Victor hit with his left club—once, twice, three times. Hobble parried. When the right club came hacking down, Hobble sidestepped and swung the staff towards Victor's left foot. In the last instance, Victor parried with his left club.

Turning, Victor swung the right club in an arc towards Hobble. The counter-attack was expected but came in faster than Hobble had anticipated. He could not jump back without revealing his less than crippled physique. In the fraction of a beat he had, he decided to counter with a strike of his own. Reversing the momentum of the staff, he twisted it upwards so that the lower end circled upward towards Victor's head. It was a desperate move.

Hobble's strike had to land first, to take the brunt out of Victor's swing. Closing his eyes, he braced for the impact. He heard a whooshing sound, like when a gust of wind finds its way down a chimney and makes the flames blaze. A jolt went up his arms as the staff connected. The swinging club made contact with his left upper arm, but there was no force behind it. A collective groan went through the crowd. Hobble opened his eyes.

Victor lay on his back several steps away. Out cold. He had a dent in his head. The left part of the man's face was broken. The left eye bulged.

Hobble's stare shifted from the man to the staff and back again. No, no, no. Not this again. *Troll balls, not this shit again!* For several moments everything was still, all was quiet. And then, all of a sudden, the world restarted. The people in the crowd started talking. Some shook their heads, others held hands in front of their mouths. Others laughed and pointed. Some at Victor, some at Hobble. Faster looked from Victor to Hobble, his mouth hanging open.

'Seize him!' someone shouted. 'He has broken the rules. The law! Take that criminal!'

Chapter 34: Third party

Gilmir sat at his table, waiting for Saendar. When the old man came in, he glanced around the room before he started towards Gilmir. With deliberate steps, he navigated between tables, people and chairs. He nodded to a few of the patrons, but when his eyes found Gilmir, he raised his eyebrows.

'I owe you an apology.' Gilmir nodded for Saendar to sit.

'You do?' Saendar asked, and pulled out a chair.

'Yes, last time we met, I had a terrible day. And I was less than gracious. I am sorry about that.'

'As I said, I was not offended. Now, I doubt that you invited me over to say sorry. What's on your mind, Darieth?'

Gilmir smiled. 'I'm called Gilmir around here, and no, I did not call this meeting just to chat. I need your help.'

'Do you, now? Do you need help from an old drunkard? One who goes around feeling sorry for himself?'

'I said I was sorry.'

Saendar held up his hand. 'You are right, the temptation was just too strong. It is not every day one such as you asks me for help. You look much better, by the way.'

'Thank you.' Gilmir glanced around the room and leaned over the table. 'Do you know what my name means?'

'Gilmir? Yes, I think I do. Star-jewel isn't it?' Saendar lowered his voice.

'Yes, it is, and I have one for sale. Moreover, I'm acquainted with someone who may be interested.'

'Okay, so what do you need from me?'

'I want you to reach out and set up a meeting. You know this place and the people who live here.'

'Meeting with whom?'

'Two of Voan's men. One of them is known as Dick, the other I call Shark. I expect them to be interested.'

'What's in it for me?'

'If the sale goes well, no disasters occur, and we receive the money and all that, your cut is one-tenth of the deal.'

'It is risky,' Saendar said, stroking his hand over his bald head. 'Doing business with Voan … If anything goes wrong, this could rebound into my face. You can always run away. I have to stay and suffer the consequences.'

'That is why you'll get paid.'

'Hmm … So if I agree to this. What else? When? Where?'

'Tomorrow is as good a day as any if you can get it done. As to where? Somewhere public but such as we can speak in private, nonetheless. And yes, you will be at the meeting as well. As the neutral third party.'

'But if I gain one-tenth, I won't be neutral.'

'Even better,' said Gilmir, smiling.

'Okay. But are you sure *you* want to operate so close to Voan?'

Gilmir stared at the old man, but Saendar met his gaze without wavering. What the old man knew or thought he knew was impossible to say. But one thing was sure, Gilmir did not want to discuss the matter with someone like Saendar. He was not going to confirm any suspicions the cripple might have, or inadvertently give him more information. 'Just set up the meeting,' Gilmir said at last, 'and let me worry about who I do, and don't do, business with.'

Saendar lifted his left hand to his brow in a mock salute. 'Yes, sir!'

Chapter 35: Hunt

Ada drifted among the spirits of Sha'ton, searching for anyone who could help her escape the dungeon. Her recent experiences, the dire circumstances and the powers of the starglass resting against her skin had greatly enhanced her ability to reach out beyond the limits of her physical being. The initial surge of optimism had faded, however, as the limitations of her magic were gradually revealed to her.

The first problem was that she did not know whom to call upon for help.

Most inhabitants of the city were commoners. Shopkeepers, maids, children, whores, brawlers and drunkards. Whom among them would be able to help, even if they wanted to?

Eavesdropping on their words, even their emotions, soon became tiresome. They were concerned about small problems, thought about inconsequential matters and gossiped mindlessly among themselves.

There were a few exceptions, though. People of power and position, that stood out like bonfires in the night among the common rabble. Ada encountered experienced bounty hunters and gladiators, elves and dwarves who had lived longer than any human, and a noblewoman who used subtle magic to charm and manipulate her peers and business partners.

Ada could listen to their words as easily as if she stood right next to them, but accessing their thoughts and feelings were far more difficult and dangerous. They were more guarded than the common people, and far more resistant to scrying magic. Furthermore, if they detected an unseen presence or an attempt at breaking through their protective barriers, any one of them might be able to counterattack in some way or another.

Sha'ton thrived on conflict and competition. Benevolent souls were few and far between, and those rare individuals rarely reached the higher echelons of the hierarchy in the city.

Ada found that going unnoticed among a crowd of people was a lonely, depressive existence. Her attempts at whispering or talking to a few isolated individuals had been unsuccessful. From their reactions, she had learned that they had noticed *something*, but could not understand her words or identify the source. Some had waved in the air, as if to chase off an insect. Others had been startled, and hastened to find the company of others. Like a child, scared by some unidentifiable sound in the night.

Manoeuvring in this state was not like walking around in the city. It was more like swimming than walking. Physical objects were different, and she could pass effortlessly through most barriers, like wooden doors and walls. Even people, though that was quite unpleasant to both Ada and the unfortunate victim. Some materials, like solid rock and thick oak, provided more resistance. Thus, Ada carefully floated along the streets, more or less following the unobstructed routes she would have if she'd been walking.

Everything looked different, too. Inverted, somehow. Things that were normally not prominent or even visible, could glow or radiate as Ada observed them. Solid objects, walls and buildings, might fade into pale, almost see-through sheets. People looked different as well. At first, Ada saw them as patches of light, some surrounded by an aura. She would recognise some by how they felt, rather than how they seemed. Now, she had learned to identify their toned-down physical characteristics, and could perceive them as beings more similar to how they would seem if she met them in the streets.

Under different circumstances, Ada might have found the experience quite thrilling. But now, her body was dying in a cold dungeon cell, and she did not have the time to explore the entire city in search of the ideal saviour. As her desperation intensified, she let curiosity guide her through the streets.

Ada felt the emanations of anger before she heard the shouting voices. She soon found half a dozen men chase a single individual through the streets, and followed them. The prey made the hunting pack work hard, by darting into side streets and alleys, knocking over tables and barrels as he ran.

Their prey was the halfling called Hobble.

Chapter 36: The Elf

Hobble sat off in the opposite direction from the approaching men. Jumping the remains of a stone wall and sliding under a wagon he came clear of the throng. He slipped down an alley. Even mid-morning, the towering buildings made the narrow street gloomy. Stalking close to the buildings, he hoped the shadows engulfed him. It was probably his imagination, but he felt the wish came true.

'Let's go, he went down here!' The call came from the alley opening.

Hobble prayed he was concealed. In the next moment, all went dark around him. *What in a crazy troll's cave!* Someone was using magic. Feeling the wall on his left, he continued forward. At least he did not have to limp to carry on the charade of the crippled foot.

'What's that darkness?' The call came from behind. 'Watch out, there is magic about!'

A few moments later, Hobble emerged from the dark globe. He glanced around and saw no one. Weighing his options, he decided to go for speed and started running down the street. Discerning that his followers would approach the darkness with caution, he concluded that he might leave them altogether if he hurried.

Rushing out in a busier street, he resumed the limping and blended with the crowd. He followed the mass for a while, but they moved too slowly for the impatient halfling. Coming to an intersection, he left the hectic street and went down an alleyway. He hobbled along at a brisk pace. Soon he was back in Oldtown and confident he had left the pursuers behind. But what now? He was a criminal. By the laws of Shacktown, he would be sentenced by one of the councilmen. He was not sure who was in charge of the area around Bits Arena, but it did not matter. The sentence would be to fight in the stadium at the weekend. It was Wednesday today. In a few days, he would fight for his life for the amusement of rich human ladies.

Unless.

Hobble came to the inn. Stepping into the common room, he nodded to the old man at the bar before he climbed the stairs to the second floor. At the third door, he raised his hand to knock. Knowing there was no turning back after entering, he hesitated. Bowing his head, he sighed and knocked.

'Come,' sounded the muffled voice from within.

Hobble opened the door. The elf looked up from some papers he had in front of him at the table.

'Hobble'—the elf raised his eyebrows—'I didn't expect to see you.'

'I need your help.'

'You realise my help does not come for free?'

'I do. May I become a part of your group?' Hobble asked.

'I will ask you this only once,' Zekatar said, 'so be sure about your reply. After having worked so hard to leave my employment. After breaking into the dungeon and getting that sickly elf out, are you sure you will come back under my dark wings?'

Hobble nodded.

Zekatar watched him, cocking his head and lifting his eyebrows.

'Yes,' Hobble said with all the conviction he could muster.

Chapter 37: Evil

'You're alive,' Zekatar said, flatly, as soon as the halfling left the room. If he felt any surprise or relief by her presence, he did not reveal it.

'*No thanks to you.*' Ada did not speak the words out loud, but her thoughts expressed their meaning clearly. She did not know how it was possible, or whether it was her powers or the drow's that allowed them to communicate in such a fashion.

'Probably not.'

'*You're evil!*'

'Do you know me so well already?'

'*You sold me for two bits!*' Ada screamed, as anger and grief overwhelmed her. Her words echoed in the dungeon.

'I'm sure you were worth them both.'

'*He killed Rayn!*' Ada kept from screaming this time, but flung her feelings at the drow. Instead of words, she conveyed her memories. Images of the attack, the fire, Rayn dying in the cell. Fear and sorrow.

'I'm sorry about your friend,' Zekatar said. Ada could not tell if he was sincere. She could not read him at all.

'*Get me out of here,*' Ada said. '*You owe me.*'

Zekatar paused, allowing Ada to calm down. He poured a drink from a decanter into a small glass, and took a sip before he replied.

'Do you know how to swim?' he said.

'*I do, why?*'

'Because that is how you leave the dungeons. Dead or alive, everybody swims in the end.'

'*That makes no sense.*'

'It will, soon enough. Just stay very still when they come.'

Chapter 38: Win-win?

'Good, you are here,' Gilmir said, turning from the window where he had been watching the street. 'Things are moving along, we have ...' He trailed off when he saw Hobble. The halfling closed the door behind him and took a seat. 'What happened?'

'A lot of things. Where to start?' Hobble said, seemingly to himself.

'At the beginning, I would suggest,' Gilmir took it upon himself to answer.

Hobble seemed annoyed for a silent moment before he cleared his throat. 'Okay, so I went to Bits, planning to lose a few matches as you suggested. I was drawn against a boy called Tommy. Perfect. He is a decent sort. No problem losing against him in any regard. But then the strange started. You know, like when women with beards and men tall as trolls come to town?'

'Is that an analogy?'

'Yes, of course. Did you think that was my story? A woman with a beard?'

'I hate analogies.'

'Why?'

'Because they are useless. You misdirect and lose important information in the process of making an analogy. In this case, you had my thoughts going in the direction of a travelling circus. Tall men and bearded women. Wasting time and effort on things that have no relevance. Please tell me what happened and skip the stupid analogies.'

Hobble stared at him.

'You were supposed to fight Tommy but then ...' Gilmir said, compelling Hobble to go on by drawing circles in the air with his hand.

Hobble shook his head. 'In the next moment, Tommy was gone, and Faster was discussing with some fellow called Victor. He then announced that this Victor had agreed to step in for Tommy. He was tall—looked the part of a real fighter. Next thing I knew, I was in the ring with him.'

'Have you ever seen this Victor before?'

'Never.'

'And then?'

'It became immediately clear that this Victor wasn't pissing around. He wanted a real fight. And I had to do all I could to keep living.'

'You are killing the suspense by being here—quite in one whole little piece!'

Hobble gave him a look before he continued. 'I found myself parrying blow after blow just to survive. And then, suddenly, I was too late. He had me beat. As a last resort, and without any hope, I countered with a blow of my own. I knew I was too late, but the weirdest thing happened. My blow connected first. Hard. Victor went down with a broken head. Everything went still. At last, it dawned on me that I had broken the rules, and I took off. All the others woke at the same moment, and some guys came after me. I ran.'

'Did you escape?' Gilmir asked, in mock horror before a grin spread over his angular face.

'You are in an annoying mood today. I liked you better when you were barely living. Remember? When I rescued you? Again and again? Smiling doesn't suit you.' Hobble rubbed his broken nose.

'I'm sorry! I'll do better,' Gilmir said, trying to stop grinning. 'Where did you go?'

'I'll come to that. The strange isn't over. I ran down a side street. Hoping the shadows would conceal me. Suddenly a globe of darkness fell over me. But the strangest thing was that nothing more happened. I crept out on the other side and ran off. Whoever is casting that darkness over me, didn't get anything out of it.'

'I'm not so sure about that.'

'How so?'

'Let's take a step back. When—'

'An analogy?' Hobble broke him off.

'No, a metaphor. It's not the same. And don't interrupt me. I had a question for you. When you cracked in Victor's head—did something else happen at the same time?'

'What do you mean?'

'Did you see something, feel something, hear something?'

Hobble went silent a moment before his eyes widened. 'How did you know?'

This time it was Gilmir giving Hobble a look.

'There was something. I heard this sound. Like when the wind comes down the chimney,' Hobble said, imitating the rush of wind with his hands. '*Whoosh.*'

'You magician!' Gilmir replied.

'What do you mean?'

'You wished for your staff to hit Victor faster than possible. It did. You wished for the shadows to conceal you and it went completely dark. I reckon there is quite a bit of magic in that tiny body of yours.'

'But I didn't do anything. I don't know any spells or incantations. I didn't mutter or wave my hands!'

'Do you know anything about magic you haven't read in children's books?'

Hobble did not answer. Gilmir continued.

'That's mostly how magic happens. Manipulating energies with your mind, if you possess the ability for it. Wind magic or light magic, you can manipulate wind and shadows. You have the makings of a moon mage in you.'

'But I haven't done anything like that before!'

'Are you sure? Maybe not that potent, but something smaller, more subtle? Hiding in shadows that were barely there? In some time of dire need perhaps? That stone of yours would aid you, making your magic more potent. Making a globe of darkness when you wanted shadows. Cracking a man's head in when you sought a fast jab.'

Hobble went pale. And silent. Gilmir let him take his time.

'So what you are saying … I know magic? I have used it before?'

'So it would seem.'

'And I can do it again. Even without the shard?'

'You probably can. Perhaps better than before. Because the stone helped you sense it more clearly. You know better how to manipulate it now, I would think.'

Hobble smiled, but his expression revealed that there was more to this story. Gilmir gave him a pause before he continued. 'So, what happened next?'

'I ran,' Hobble said, his eyes focusing again, 'If they caught me, they would surely lock me up in the dungeons until Saturday. And then some starved beast would tear me to pieces in the stadium for the pleasure of the crowd. So, I had to find another solution.'

'Not getting caught?'

'I could run from the city, but I have nowhere to go. No, I met someone. Someone who could help me.'

'Who?'

'A lanista.'

'How did that help you?'

'I don't have to spend the next days and nights in the awful dungeon. And it may get me out of the "feed-the-beast fights", and into something I could actually survive.'

'And the rose's thorn?' Gilmir kept asking.

'I am *his* gladiator. Until I have earned my freedom.'

'And how easy would you say it is to earn that, on a scale from "bloody hard" to "dating an ogre half-god"?'

'Let's just say owing that crazy dwarf doesn't compare to this.'

'Good.'

'Good? Why in the name of all fallen gods do you deem this a good thing?'

'I reckon that before we see the end of this, I've had the chance to save you a sufficient number times to call it even,' Gilmir said, smiling.

Hobble stared back at him, apparently unable to see the humour in the situation. Gilmir decided to help him. 'Or, and this is a distinct possibility I am sure, you will be dead, and I will be free of all obligations. It is a win-win situation for me. No, sorry, that was a bit discourteous of me. Truth be told, it is more of a "win-break-even" situation. And that's better than I have been used to the last few months!'

'Balls, I miss the time when you were too sick to speak. I hope this mood of yours gets gutted and fed to the rats!'

Gilmir grinned, and felt more alive than he had for ages.

Chapter 39: Rats

'Get away from her!'

Ada kicked wildly in the direction of the sickening sound, as she had done so many times since Rayn passed away. Every time Ada dozed, she awoke to the sound of rats feasting on her friend's body.

In the utter darkness of the cell, her eyes were of no use. Instead, other senses were sharpened. She heard tiny claws scrape against the stone as the rats approached the dead half-elf. The awful sound of sharp teeth piercing her skin, ripping crumb-sized chunks of flesh from her. There were softer sounds as well, all the more disturbing.

The smell from the corpse added a subtle nuance to the foul odour of mould and excrements. Her skin was cold and numb, despite her routine of standing up, bending and stretching as much as the short chains would allow her. If she ever got out of this place alive, she would have to be strong enough to walk on her own.

Ada never thought she would be desperate enough to lick moisture off the walls or eat a rat. She had done that, and worse. Similar to how she sometimes channelled fire from her surroundings through herself, necessity taught her to extract moisture from the damp cell. Ada would catch a rat as it tried to take a bite of her, and hold it firmly in her fist. It would squirm in her hand as she slowly absorbed the water. In the corner behind her, there was a stack of dried rats. In case she ever felt hungry enough for it to be worth the effort of chewing them.

However, rat meat and magically extracted water were not enough to nourish her through weeks in the cold dungeon. Or was it only days? No, it had to be weeks. Ada clutched the shard in her hand. It was fading, as she had been drawing from its power to sustain herself, to stay alive.

Ada had benefited from her shard's enhancing abilities to draw heat from her surroundings, keeping her warm enough to avoid shivering. As thirst, hunger and despair overwhelmed her, she drew energy directly from the shard. Draining its essence of life, as she had been draining water from the rats.

Soon, the powers in Ada's shard would be depleted as well, and her soul would depart to wherever souls go. Leaving her weak body behind, another feast for the rats.

She would have to find a way to escape. There must be someone who could help.

In the dark dungeon below the city of Sha'ton, Ada lowered the barriers separating herself from the world outside. Her spirit naked and vulnerable, she reached out for someone—anyone—who could help her.

'I'm dying. Find me.'

Chapter 40: Alley

'Is the night market still around?' Gilmir said, looking down on his tattered clothes.

'Yeah, Wednesdays and Saturdays. Why?' Hobble said, looking up from the pieces of cloth, he was stitching together.

'Do you have a few coins to spare?'

'I have a few coins. The end.'

'I am well aware funds are low and I need to start paying for myself. And I will be able to do that if I can get a set of clothing that doesn't make me look like a human beggar.'

'How about an elf beggar?'

'There is no such thing.'

'Why?'

'An elf would find a way. He would leave the city and find food. He would rather die than beg.'

'And if I said no?'

'I would kill you and take the money,' Gilmir said, smiling.

Hobble grunted and fished out a few coins, tossing them to Gilmir.

'Thank you,' the elf said, catching the coins. For the first time, he studied the piece Hobble was working on. He cocked his head. 'Has your lanista asked you to play the part of a pirate on Saturday?'

Hobble did not answer but took up the eyepatch he had been fitting to a string and tried it on. He gazed, with one eye, at the elf for a few beats before he broke the silence.

'Do you know why pirates use eyepatches, Stick Man?'

The question took Gilmir off guard. Eyepatches were common among pirates, and Gilmir, although he had not contemplated the reason, had assumed eye injuries were a typical hazard in that line of occupation. However, when forced to think about it … Why would eye injuries be more common for pirates?

'Yes, mister know-it-all, why do pirates wear eyepatches?' Hobble pressed, clearly enjoying the elf's hesitation.

'It's hard for me to explain human behaviour, but I was led to believe it was used to cover an injury or a missing eye.'

'You were "led to believe"? Do you know anything about pirates you haven't learned from children's books?'

Gilmir would not dignify that with an answer.

'Let me teach you something, my naive friend,' Hobble said, 'Humans and halflings don't see especially well in darkness. At least not until their eyes have fully adjusted to the lighting conditions. So, for instance, when a pirate is fighting out on the deck and then needs to step below deck for more fighting, his eyes need time to adjust from the light on deck to the darkness below. However, if he wears an eyepatch, he could just remove that, or even better, switch it to the other eye, and utilise his adjusted eyesight. In other words, an eyepatch may come in handy if you are going from the light to the dark and vice versa. Hence, I like to have one at hand.'

'In other words, humans, and evidently halflings, need them to compensate for their suboptimal functioning?' Gilmir asked.

'Oh, no, no, no. I won't let you turn the table on this one, elf! The point is that you had no clue whatsoever of why pirates wear eyepatches, and I needed to school you.' Hobble waggled a finger in front of him.

'Call it what you will. The fact is that you, and your human friends, wear patches because your eyes don't work properly! But I am happy you take your precautions, halfling. Better to look silly with a patch, than to be blind and dead without one, I guess!'

With that, Gilmir turned and walked out the door.

Later that evening, Gilmir was making his way back from the market. Under his arm, he carried a shirt and a pair of trousers. The clothes were not of high quality, and not even new, but much better than what he was wearing. Turning a corner, he started down a quiet street. A woman shouted something, and Gilmir shifted his gaze towards the sound. Down in an alley, three shapes were visible, and it soon became clear there was some disagreement. The alley smelled of piss and rotten fruit. Gilmir continued on his way, leaving the troublemakers to their own.

'Leave me alone,' the woman called, and something with the voice made Gilmir pause.

He turned and stalked down the alley. Behind some barrels and crates, he could see a woman hitting a man. But before she could break away, the other man caught her from behind, pinning her arms to her body in a bear hug.

'Help!' the woman yelled, 'Help me!'

The man holding her heaved her around, so they both faced the other man. This one wiped a hand under his bloodied nose, glanced at it, and smiled. 'Nosebleed' was a brute of a man. Barrel-chested and broad of shoulders. Black, unkempt hair protruded from his head in every direction. He moved with ease, if not very fast. Probably a bouncer and a real danger if he could get his hands on you. His companion, 'Bear Hug', was smaller, dirtier and with huge forearms. Maybe a butcher.

'I like a woman with spirit,' Nosebleed said, closing in on the girl once more.

Gilmir glanced around, found an almost clean crate, turned it on the side and carefully lay his new clothes on it. Then he stepped out in the dim light from the torches in the street.

'Let her go.'

Nosebleed shifted his gaze to Gilmir and studied him from head to toe and back again. The two others turned, Bear Hug still holding the woman. The familiar woman.

'Move along, beggar,' Nosebleed said.

'Gilmir!' Chris said, 'Run, get help!'

The two brutes exchanged nervous glances and Nosebleed took a step forward.

'Let her go, and I won't tell anyone,' Gilmir said.

Nosebleed, who kept walking towards Gilmir, laughed. Suddenly, he lunged forward, grabbing at the elf. Gilmir stepped aside and pushed the grasping hand to the side. After regaining his balance, Nosebleed cocked his head and seemed to look at Gilmir in a new light.

'We can still settle this without anyone getting hurt,' Gilmir said, 'Let the girl go.'

'I don't think so. This is your last chance of leaving this place in one piece,' said Nosebleed.

'Finish him,' Bear Hug said, 'I am getting tired of this.'

Nosebleed came on again. Fist swinging. Gilmir ducked and stepped inside the range of the muscular man's arms. Coming in from the side, the elf drove his right fist up into the man's kidney, and stepped back out. Nosebleed doubled over, gasping. But not for long. Soon he came in again leading with a wild swing with his right fist. Gilmir stepped to the side, caught the fist with his right hand and turned with it. With his back to the man, he stabbed his left thumb into the soft spot between the man's thumb and hand. Finding the nerve, he pressed with all his strength. The man moaned and fell to his knees. Gilmir turned, twisting Nosebleed's arm until the man lay flat on his back. With his foot to the man's throat, he glanced over at Bear Hug.

'Let her go, and you will both live,' the elf said.

Bear Hug and Chris both gaped at him. The girl came to her senses first and broke free. Gilmir let go of Nosebleed, took Chris by the arm and started walking away. Over his shoulder, he spoke.

'If you ever bother this girl again I'll hunt you down. Next time you won't see me coming.'

Gilmir fished up his new clothes on the way. Chris kept looking back while they headed out of the alley. Coming out into the street, she looked at Gilmir.

'How did you do that?'

'Do what?'

'Take out the big brute like that. He must have been double your weight.'

'Consider it your first lesson. Weight is hardly a factor in fighting,' Gilmir said, smiling. 'This one's for free.'

'But you barely hit him!'

'I don't much like fist fights. Do you know what hitting a man like that in the face feels like?'

'In fact, I do!' Chris glanced down on her hand and shook it, before grinning at the elf.

'Indeed, you do!' Gilmir said, and chuckled.

Chris laughed.

'This is me,' Chris said a few moments later, tilting her head towards a worn-down building. They were barely a block from the inn.

'Are you ready for your second lesson tomorrow? Mid-morning?'

'I don't have much money,' Chris said, looking at her feet.

'You can pay what you can afford. You know the clearing out by the graveyard?'

'Sure.'

'Great. I'll be wearing my best clothes.' Gilmir held up his bundle.

'I am sure it will be an improvement!'

Chapter 41: Marble

Ada leaned back against the wall. It used to be cold, but not anymore. Instead, she felt oddly warm inside. And tired, so tired.

'*Find me, Gilmir.*'

She knew it wouldn't work, no matter how hard she tried. Or how many times she tried. Even in his sleep, his mental barriers were up. When he was awake, she couldn't even find him. His mind was guarded.

Ada had tried communicating with the elf as she had with the drow, conveying images and emotions rather than spoken words. Again, she projected what her senses told her about the cell. The cold, the sound of the rats, the smell of mould and decaying, human flesh.

She dosed and drifted away, leaving the dungeon and Sha'ton. Floating through the air, drawn towards something she did not know or understand. A warm wind enveloped her like a woollen blanket, comforting her.

Ada opened her eyes, and entered the gate of a beautiful city of gold and marble. Warm and clean. There was soft music, and laughter. Fair elves walked in the streets, smiling and singing. Everything was perfect.

'Come,' the wind beckoned.

Ada obeyed, until she stood in front of the long, polished steps of a marble palace, leading to an arched entrance on the third floor. Servants opened the tall double doors for her as she approached, and bowed for her as she entered the spacious audience hall.

In the centre of the round chamber, stood a huge starfall shard, taller than any man. Ada felt its immense power embrace her, remedying her aches and sorrows. Like a warm bath after a cold night out in the streets, but better. Much better.

Ada fell to her knees before the gigantic starglass. She reached out with her hands but did not dare touch it.

Movement caught her attention, distracting her from relishing the moment. Ada lifted her gaze, and saw a tall elf raising up from a throne behind the starglass. His blue eyes sparkled, like the sea on a beautiful summer day.

'Welcome, Ada,' he said, his voice gentle and melodious. 'I've been waiting for you.'

Chapter 42: Fencing

Gilmir woke early. During the night he had dreamt about Ada. She had been in a cell. Calling for help. He could not remember much more. It was probably a mix of his time in the dungeons and Chris calling from help the night before. Still, the sounds and smells, the cold walls, the details were vivid in his mind.

He pushed the images away.

It would be a busy day. A fine day. He dressed with a smile on his face and moved the chair to the window. Putting his feet on the sill, he started detailing the plan in his mind. Saendar had delivered a message to Hobble. The old man had arranged the meeting with Dick and Shark. They would meet at the church square at sundown. Getting rid of the tainted shard would be a wise move. He hoped Hobble would not get cold feet. The halfling had been strange about the stone. One could not carry such shards without being influenced by it one way or another. Especially if one had an untrained mind.

Moreover, this stone was foul. Its impact would be bad. Gilmir put the thoughts to the back of his mind. It was no use worrying about it. They would learn the truth soon enough. Before that, he would meet with Chris. It would be good to get some weapons training. It was months since the last time he had done any work in that department. Gilmir stretched and watched the first rays of sunshine, reaching the slanted roofs of Oldtown.

*

'It is all good leading with your left foot sometimes, or even most of the time, but you must be able to adapt,' Gilmir said, reaching out a hand and helping Chris to her feet.

'That's how my father taught me!' Chris answered.

'I know. That is how humans with rapiers fight. Jumping back and forth on a line. It is great for attacking straight ahead and defending by skipping backwards. However, as I just demonstrated, your enemy may not attack in a straight line.'

'I was too slow, try that again and I'll show you,' Chris said with determination.

'With pleasure, fencer!'

Gilmir crouched and raised his two wooden swords. He had made the two practice swords that same morning, in addition to one resembling a rapier for Chris. They had been sparring for half an hour. The girl was talented. Fast and strong. However, her former teacher was no swordsman. A fencer? Yes. A fighter? Probably. But a swordsman? No. A swordsman would not limit himself to one style, at least not if the style was so inefficient.

Chris quick-stepped forward. Three steps and a lunge. Gilmir parried with his shorter blade and stabbed with his long blade. Chris reversed momentum and stepped back, avoiding the hit. They continued this for a while, the girl working her legs furiously, back and forth, back and forth. The elf more economical in his movement, a small sidestep here, a parry there. Chris came forward again. This time Gilmir slapped the sword away. The girl half turned following her blade and the elf sidestepped the other way. Chris spun around, but too slow. By the time she turned, two wooden practice swords were pointing at her chest. She breathed heavily.

'You are in better shape than me.'

Gilmir laughed. 'The other day, I was a tired old man, and now I am in better shape?'

'I am exhausted; you are hardly breathing!'

'I couldn't have kept up with all that jumping around. I move less.'

'How can you defeat me so easily by moving less?'

'My technique, my experience, but most of all, my style of fighting.'

'So your point is that I shouldn't lead with my right foot?'

'I keep telling you, don't I?'

Chris shook her head, looking annoyed.

'So what happened this time?' Gilmir asked. 'You kept up as long as I let you fight on the straight line. But as soon as I stepped to the side, your quick-stepping couldn't help you anymore, and I had you beat.'

'I got fatigued. I should have been able to turn in time. You fight dirty!'

'So you think the cornerstones of this world of ours are princes and fair fights?'

'No, no, I know you are right, I'm drained and discouraged. I thought I was good at this. I have been practising for a long time, you know. Then you come along, beating me without breaking a sweat. It's just … hard.'

'Did I say you weren't good at this? You are incredibly fast and strong. Really talented, but you need to trust me when I say your garden fencing style won't bring you far in this world of unfair fights and hideous brutes.'

Chris smiled. 'You think I'm good?'

Gilmir almost regretted the words. Letting a novice fighter think she was good was the worst you could do. However, he had shown her she was not *that* good. He trusted a few words of encouragement would not ruin her. However, before he could say something Chris continued.

'I trust you. You have shown me that you are right. So where do we start?'

'Oh, I think that is enough for your first, I mean second, lesson. We have come to an important understanding here. Tomorrow we can start working on your new pose.'

'Tired, old man?'

'Tired? Yes. Old? No. Man? Definitely not!'

Chris chuckled.

Chapter 43: Selling

The sun was setting when Gilmir and Hobble walked out on Church Square, where the old elven architecture was more prominent. The gnome clock in the old belfry showed the time to be nine hours and a quartermark. Gilmir glanced at Hobble. One eye was covered by the eyepatch. The small thief limped along, using his staff for support. How he was able to deform his foot at will without it hampering him in other situations was beyond the elf. Was this another aspect where the halfling used magic without knowing it?

'Are you comfortable selling the stone?'

'As long as you find me another, I am quite happy.'

'Find you another? Me?'

'Yes, I've got the taste for it now. It's like when you taste good wine for the first time, after drinking grape juice for ages.'

'Another analogy?'

'Sure, I will stop when I get another stone!'

'Let's sell this one first!'

'Sure. In the meantime, I'll be like an itch you cannot reach.'

'Stop it.'

Hobble chuckled. 'By the way, ain't you afraid that the two thugs will recognise you? From when you distracted them in the forest, I mean?'

'No.'

'Why?'

'You'll see.'

Hobble shrugged. 'Just don't expect me to be saving your ass again. I refuse to be further ahead in that race.'

'Don't worry, unlike when we met, I am now capable of saving my own behind.'

Saendar stood on by the corner of the towering church in the east, waving them over. There was no sign of Dick and Shark. Gilmir scanned the area while they closed the distance to the old man. Some people were still on the square. A cobbler had a little stand by an old fountain, which was not working any more. In a few other booths, people were tidying away their wares.

By the stairs to the church, a busker stood singing and playing the lute. Three men stood by an empty booth talking and occasionally glancing in the direction of Gilmir and Hobble.

'Do you know any of those men by that empty booth?' Gilmir whispered.

Hobble did not look straight away. Instead, he took his time looking casually around before he glanced over at the men. 'No, I don't think so.'

Saendar smiled when they reached him. 'Welcome, fine gentlemen! I see the world hasn't been too unkind to you lately.'

'Good evening, Saendar,' Gilmir said. 'Everything all right?'

'I would say so. Your potential buyers are waiting right around the corner.'

'They are alone?'

'Yes, as far as I can determine, they are.'

'Good, let's go.'

Saendar took them around the corner and down a narrow street. The tall buildings made the alley gloomy. If the humans planned an ambush on an elf in the dark, they were idiots. Gilmir glanced at Hobble. The little fellow shifted the pad to his other eye. Still not sure if the halfling was messing with him or that trick really worked, Gilmir smiled and shook his head.

'Right ahead,' Saendar said.

Gilmir shifted his focus down the alley. Better not to underestimate the two thugs. Under a small roof, probably a side entrance to the church, he spotted the two men. Scanning the surrounding area he could see a hundred places for people to hide. He looked behind but saw no one. This was not the public place he had instructed Saendar to find. Gilmir glanced at the old cripple. The short man seemed perfectly at ease. Too much so?

'Good afternoon, Dick,' Gilmir said, locking his eyes on the man.

Dick and Shark came forward. The short and bald Dick had a black eye and a cut on his cheek, Shark had a split lip over his crooked teeth and a swollen forehead.

'Let's see it,' Dick said.

'It seems you've had a rough time. I am sorry about that,' Gilmir said and nodded to Hobble. The halfling took the shard out.

Shark held out a hand, and Hobble glanced at Gilmir before handing the stone over. The man held the shard up to the meagre light and studied it.

'It's the real thing,' Gilmir said, 'and it will be yours for one hundred silver pieces. The quality is not the best, so you will get it at this generous price. A one-time offer.'

Shark continued to study it, while Dick glanced from Hobble to Saendar.

'You can have seventy-five pieces for it,' Shark said, lowering the stone.

'No, I am not doing any stupid human haggling. Our price is a hundred pieces. Take it or leave it.'

Hobble glanced at Gilmir, and Shark looked at Dick. The bald man shifted his feet and gave a small nod.

This was too easy.

'And one more thing,' Gilmir said, 'some time ago there was an elf imprisoned in the dungeons. He had two swords. Elven swords. I want them.'

Dick and Shark exchanged glances again. 'If I'm not mistaken, those swords are in the hands of councilman Voan now. Out of our reach,' Shark said.

'Hmm … Alright, fair enough, Shark,' Gilmir replied, using the nickname he had only ever used in the glade in the forest when Hobble had stolen the shard. The shard Gilmir now was carrying under his shirt. There was a flicker of something in Shark's eyes, but it disappeared.

'Pay them,' Shark said to Dick. The bald man took out two pouches and threw them over. Hobble and Gilmir caught one each and peeked inside.

'Very well, then,' Saendar said, 'everything seems to be in order. I call this deal settled.'

Dick and Shark nodded and drew back. Hobble, Gilmir and Saendar went the other way. Coming around the corner and out on Church Square once again, Gilmir broke the silence.

'Thank you, Saendar.' He gave the cripple ten silver pieces. 'Come by the inn tomorrow and I'll give you a chance to earn some more. And this time I'll even buy you a drink.'

'That's most gracious of you, sir! I'll see you tomorrow,' Saendar said and broke off to the left. Probably in the direction of the closest place to where he could spend his newly earned coins.

'So, elves don't haggle?' Hobble asked.

'Of course we do.'

'So, what was that?'

'I had to find out.'

'Find out what?'

'If Voan knows about me,' Gilmir said.

'Explain yourself, elf, this is like talking to a giant guarding a bridge.'

'Something was off with that meeting. They should have recognised me, and that should have yielded a reaction of some sort.'

'Maybe they're not very observant?'

'No, that Shark fellow pays attention. Besides, they agreed to the price all too easily. They didn't react to the part about the swords either. Even told me where I could find them. And, last but not least, he didn't react when I called him Shark.'

'So, what does this all mean?'

'I am not sure. However, I do know that Voan knows I am out. And, at some point, he will come for me. Perhaps this was the last proof he needed.'

'What are you going to do?'

'I'll spare him the trouble, and go to him instead.'

'Are you sure? That's insane!' Hobble said.

'I'm glad you like it. For you are coming as well.'

'Me? I already have a crazy dwarf and a cynical dark elf on my back, I am not sure I need more.'

'You know what they say about multiple enemies?'

'No, never heard.'

'It is better with three enemies in front of you than one at your back.'

'Technically, I had two in front of me, and then you dragged in the third.'

'Let's not get into semantics!' Gilmir said, smiling.

Hobble shook his head, and they continued in silence.

Chapter 44: Wind

Ada listened absently as the rats went about their business. She had stopped trying to repel them by kicking or shouting. In fact, their presence provided some kind of comfort. The mere sound of a living creature helped remind her that she lived, that she was not alone. That she was not losing herself in the nothingness.

She felt no anger towards them, not any more. Such emotions served no purpose. There was no justice or mercy in this world. Her friend died because she got in the way of someone stronger than herself. The rats were chewing at her flesh because it was their nature. The strong will feed off the weak, and the living will feed off the dead. Nothing was right or wrong. Except for power. Power was always right. Might defined right.

Ada had wielded power, felt it surge through her, felt the ecstasy as she unleashed fire from her own hands. The shard catalysed and multiplied her powers. Now it was all but spent, pulsating slowly with the faintest hint of radiance. One last time, Ada pressed the stone against her heart, reaching out.

A warm draft gently stroked her naked arms and neck. She shivered from the touch. Ada's heart quickened.

'Live,' the wind whispered.

'You found me!' Ada gasped.

She smiled as its warm presence embraced her cold skin, like the first southern wind in spring.

'I need you,' the wind said.

Blood rose to her cheeks, thawing her face. 'I need you, too,' she said. It was true, though she never knew until now.

'I will send for you.'

'I will be ready.' In delight, Ada squeezed the starfall shard and absorbed the remaining energy.

The shard dissolved into fine powder between her fingers. Ada didn't mind.

He had found her.

Chapter 45: Information

The next day Gilmir sat at the corner table waiting for Saendar. Life was steadily improving, he decided, pouring a glass of wine. It was a dark red. He swirled the wine around in the glass and lifted it to his nose. A bouquet of vanilla. He took a sip and closed his eyes. Jammy, silky and with a hint of dark cave. Gilmir did not consider himself overly concerned with wealth, but falling stars, it was great to be able to afford decent wine.

Someone was coming. Careful steps with a slight shuffling.

'I owe you a glass of wine, Saendar.' Gilmir opened his eyes.

'You do,' the old man said, pulling out a chair, 'and I'll try to be more grateful than you were.'

'And I'll try to serve better wine.' Gilmir waved Chris over. 'Do you have a glass for Saendar? I should probably not drink the whole bottle by myself.'

'I sure do,' Chris said, smiling to the old man. 'Kind of you to take care of our lost elf here, Saendar.' The young woman winked and turned for the bar.

They sat in silence until Chris returned with the glass. Gilmir poured and gave the glass to the old man. Saendar took a sip and smiled.

'This is indeed better than the one we shared last time.'

'I am glad you agree, it would be a shame to have to kill you now,' Gilmir said and smiled.

'I know too much about you to laugh at such a joke. What can I do for you, Gilmir?'

Gilmir's smile fell away. 'I need information.'

'What sort of information?'

'The sort that comes with a price. I'll be going to get my swords back. As such, I need all the information I can get on Voan and his castle.'

'I see.'

'Well?'

'I am considering it, elf. On one side, I don't much like Voan. On the other hand, this is not just information that comes with a price. This is information that could kill.' Saendar rubbed at the stump of his right arm.

'You don't strike me as a man who shies away from a little danger. But I'll be more specific. I need to know where Voan keeps my swords and how to get there. Besides, I need to know if he has any weaknesses.'

'All right, this is what I know.' Saendar looked around the room before he continued. 'Rumour has it that there are some display cases in his throne room. If the councilman has your swords, I guess he'll keep them on display. The throne room is at the top of the castle. You know the giant glass windows you can see at the top of the building?' Saendar took a mouthful of wine. 'That would be my best guess. As to his weaknesses, by all reports, he is strong and fast, and quite handy with a blade. However, he has an injured hand, or at least he keeps the hand tucked away under his clothes.' The old man paused and seemed to consider his next words. "And there is something else. He wears a mask covering his nose and mouth when he is out, and there is always some sort of priest with him. Finally, there are some rumours, but now we are down to the stuff that I consider the most unreliable facts.'

'Let's hear it.'

'There are some rumours that he is some sort of hybrid. Part human, part reptile. Others say he is a demon or half a demon.' Saendar took another sip of wine. 'I doubt I'll be able to gather more reliable information on this.'

'Alright, thank you, that will do. Now, I just need one more thing.'

'What's that?'

'A map or instructions on how to get from the dungeons to the throne room. Preferably the best such route in terms of not being seen.'

'That will be harder.'

'I know, and that's why I'll pay you.'

'When do you need it?'

'Tomorrow?'

'I'll see what I can do.'

'Good, you know where to find me.'

Saendar stood, emptied the glass and nodded to Gilmir. 'Thank you for the wine.' After a few steps, he turned. 'Are you sure this is what you want?'

Gilmir studied the old man. There was more to the question. A warning? It did not matter. He was indeed sure. 'Yes,' he said simply.

Saendar shrugged and started to turn.

'One more thing,' Gilmir said, 'Have you heard something about two girls—one human and one half-elf?'

'The witches?'

'Possibly.'

'They started a fire in the inn a few days ago. I don't know the details, but I think they were taken in. Probably in the dungeons by now. Do you want me to look into it?'

'No, it just means I have even less time.'

'I'll get on with my part!' Saendar said and left for the door.

Gilmir shifted his gaze back to the glass in his hand. Blocking out the rest of the world, he swirled the wine and brought it to his nose. This wine really was decent.

Chapter 46: Path

Gilmir came into the sewer canal under the dungeons the same way he had exited. Before he left, he bade Chris tell Tracks to be at the stadium and look for Hobble. The wheels were turning, now he just had to hang on. Saendar had provided him with instructions and a crude map. Gilmir was impressed with how much and how detailed information the old crippling had been able to gather. That worried him as he approached the place where he had fallen down from the trapdoor in the dungeon proper.

The smell was worse than he remembered, but this time he did not need to bathe in the sludge. He hoped. Glancing up to the trapdoor, he considered his options. Saendar had provided him with another way in. However, he wanted to go through the dungeons. For several reasons, one being the fact that he did not want to rely on the old man's information more than needed.

The curved tunnel walls were made of coarse bricks. He would have to climb to reach the hatch. Such a climb he had not done in years. Studying the domed tunnel ceiling, he took off his shoes. He located the roughest stones and the largest crease and planned the challenging climb. Delving into the magic of his shard, he made his body lighter, transmitting his mass to stones on the floor. With his shoes between his teeth, he began the climb. Soon he was upside down and closing on the hatch.

He resisted the temptation to let go with his feet and hang from his fingers while he took hold of the hatch. Instead, he pressed into the wall, suspending between his hand- and footholds. His muscles ached while he scaled the last inches. At last, he reached the hatch. With his left hand, he pulled on the latch. His feet started shaking with the strain and his arms burned. Pushing forward, he reached up under the opened hatch door. Somehow, he found handholds and could pull himself up into the dungeon proper.

He rested with his back against the wall for a hundred beats. Slipping on his soft leather shoes, he moved down the hall until he came to the intersection. Through the doorway to his right, he would find his old prison wing. The familiar sounds reached him. Men moaning and whimpering. Sobbing and crying. The guards laughing in the guardroom. The smell was different from the sewer below, but no less foul. It reeked of death and decay. One hundred and twenty-four steps would take him back to his old cell. But that was not the chamber he was looking for. Ada was trapped and dying, in a cell in this very dungeon.

Footsteps sounded from the hallway to the right. Gilmir melted into the shadows by the doorway. The precise but heavy steps came closer before they stopped and started receding. Glancing around the corner, Gilmir could confirm what he already knew. Magnus, the tall Northman guard, was making his round. Gilmir recognised the sounds of every guard who had made rounds in this hellhole for the two and a half years he was locked up. All thirty-seven of them. Looking at the back of this man, Gilmir found his knife in his hand. Of all the thirty-seven guards, this man in front of him was the worst. By a bowshot. The elf stalked out into the corridor.

Silently, he closed in on the broad-shouldered man. For a moment, Gilmir considered not killing the brute. The thought caught him off guard. A few years ago, or a few months ago, no, even a week before, he would not have contemplated the option. Times had changed. He had changed. However, that would not help Magnus. The world would be a better place without him. He would not do this for himself. He did this for every other person who had, and who would have, crossed path with the Northman.

At least, that was what he told himself.

To the guard's credit, he realised something was wrong before Gilmir's dagger found his kidney. However, all he managed to do was to stop walking. Gilmir drove the blade in low, but at an upward angle, finishing with a twist, before he yanked it out. His left hand over Magnus's mouth, muffling the cry, he guided the limp body to the floor. Dragging the Northman by his blond hair, Gilmir went back towards his old cell. Some prisoners called out to him, but he ignored them. Thankfully, they had the wits to keep their voices low. Finding his old cell empty, Gilmir smiled and hauled the heavy body inside.

He was reckless, but he did not care. Something had to be done. Some people had to die.

Realising the prisoners would raise their voices if they saw him going by again, Gilmir reached out with his magic and snuffed out a torch, and then another. He waited while the prisoners reacted to the alteration. Standing there by his old cell door, memories came flowing back. Memories of endless hours lying on the floor, of starving and thirsting. Of pain and suffering. Of his mind wandering and getting lost. A shudder went through him. Last time he was here he was dying. That was no exaggeration. *Still, you are coming back. Like a beaten dog creeping back to its cruel master.* That old voice again. The one that always seemed to find him in his darkest hours. Now it came creeping back. Now that he was back in the place where he thought he would draw his last breath.

He shook his head. And moved into the shadows.

He stalked towards the guardroom. A few moments later, he was closing in on Ada's cell. He could not say precisely how he knew. It was something with the sensations and feelings he had felt in the dream. The sense of death and despair, the sound of water dripping from somewhere, the smell of rodents and their droppings.

The cell was silent. Too silent. He was too late.

Coming to the cell door, he saw the cell was empty. That could only mean one thing. *Useless. That is what you are. You can tell yourself you have changed. But you cannot save anyone. The only skill you have is killing. Stop fooling yourself. Once a killer, always a killer.* Gilmir growled. He had to agree. However, if he was to change, if he was to lead another life, he had to learn. He had to adapt.

Nevertheless, in that instance, he had no idea where Ada was or how he could help her. There was just one path ahead of him.

Pushing Ada to the back of his mind, he went on.

At the door to the guardroom, he crept up to the wall. Once again, he snuffed out two torches in the corridor. It was one of the first magic tricks he had learned in his training. The hallway went almost entirely dark. As expected, the prisoners called out. One torch went out often enough. Two torches at the same time was not that strange. But four? From inside the door, Gilmir heard grumbling and the shuffling of a chair. The next moment the door went up.

'What the …' the voice said. It was Owen, the chubby guard. 'Magnus? What's going on down there?'

No response. Owen grumbled, and feet shuffled. Soon Owen came back and out in the corridor with a torch. 'Magnus? What shit are you up to?'

As soon as Owen moved a few feet down the corridor, Gilmir slipped in the door. It was stadium day, and if things had not changed a lot, there would not be more guards nearby. Gilmir crossed the empty room. Hopefully, the sleeping quarters would also be empty, or close to. Hearing nothing at the door, he opened it and peered inside. All was still, all was quiet. He crossed the room and found the stairs. Coming up on the next floor, he should be close to the entrance to the servant's corridor. He found the secret door behind the curtain where Saendar had told him it was. It was supposed to be a short walk to the stairwell. The stairs would take him to the top of the castle. From there, it should be straightforward to find the servants entrance to the throne room.

The information proved true. Down to the smallest detail. Gilmir did not even see a servant while he made his way from the dungeons to the throne room floor at the top of the castle. This was not right. His instincts screamed at him from the back of his mind. Like a crazy little monkey. There should have been someone in his way.

He ignored his instincts. Disregarded the screaming ape.

Gilmir opened the door to the throne room.

Chapter 47: Pyre

Somewhere, far away, there was a sound.

It was a pleasant sound, almost comforting. The somewhat prolonged sound of two soft objects colliding. A heavy, soft object hitting a wet surface. Like a limp body landing in a body of water. A pool, or a river.

She fell for a moment. Then she, too, landed in the sewer.

Ada awoke and gasped for air. She immediately wished she had not done that. Her limbs, weakened by starvation and inaction, were flailing futilely as she tried to reach the surface. Her body tried to inhale and vomit simultaneously, failing at both. Unable to coordinate her movements, she resigned and allowed the current to carry her.

Did I survive on rats, only to drown in a river of piss?

As the putrid stream accelerated, the turbulent flow of the sewer brought her upper body to the surface. She suppressed the urge to breathe until she had coughed once and managed a hasty inhale before she was submerged again. That only made things worse, as the remains of sewage from her previous attempt at breathing underwater was pulled further down towards her lungs along with the small amount of air she'd caught. Again, she was stuck between the urge to inhale and the necessity of removing the contents from her lungs. As her body fought this internal battle, she was unable to swim to the surface.

Help sometimes comes in the most unexpected ways. Centuries ago, a gate of vertical metal bars had been built across the sewer, as a means to prevent enemies and sappers from entering the city of Sha'ton. As the current slammed Ada into those rusted bars, the air was forcefully expelled from her lungs, more effectively than any cough she was able to produce. Grabbing hold of the grime-covered bars, she regained her composure and control of her breathing.

In the dim light of the sewer tunnel, she looked around and took stock of her surroundings. There was no going back unless she was able to swim against the current for who knows how far. She considered squeezing her sickly, thin body between the bars but realised that her head would be too broad.

'I'm sorry I pulled you into this mess,' Ada said, as she found Rayn's body two feet away from her. Most of it was submerged, thankfully. There was a dead dog as well.

'Just the three of us, then,' Ada said.

It felt good to talk and even better to see. Above, there were holes around each bar, slightly wider than the bars themselves.

'Let's rest here for a while,' she said, 'until they open the gates and let us continue our journey. If this gate was shut permanently, there would be more of us down here.'

Half an hour later, a loud clang sounded. Soon, the metal bars stirred, and rusted wheels and chained squeaked somewhere in the wall. Slowly, the portcullis rose until the bottom spikes hung a foot above the surface. Ada made sure her travelling companions were loose from the bars before she let go and followed them wherever the sewer would take them.

'We'll probably end up in the river, eventually,' Ada said, assuming the role of the cicerone of their party. 'It will be cold, but once we get some distance from the sewer outlet, we will be able to wash off this filth and look presentable again.'

The first hints of daylight and a gust of wind indicated that she was right. The sewer passage ended in a six-foot drop into the river. Ada grabbed Rayn and the dog, and let the river carry them a quarter of a mile downstream before she found a suitable spot to climb up on to the northern bank, keeping the river between herself and anyone travelling on the road to Sha'ton.

Ada revelled in the morning sunlight and the cold air. After she had pulled her two companions out of the river, she waded back into the water to wash herself and her clothes thoroughly. She drank a few delicious mouthfuls but resisted the urge to drink more. The dangers of eating and drinking after prolonged starvation were well known and in a land frequently exposed to failed harvests, pillaging armies and sieges.

Standing in the freezing river, Ada frowned as she examined her body. There were cuts and wounds everywhere. Apparently, the rats had nibbled at her as well, and the ride down the sewer and river had not been gentle. More worrisome, her ribs and bones were clearly visible under her thin skin. As she rinsed her hair, some of it fell off and stuck between her fingers.

'Wouldn't earn a copper in a brothel looking like this,' she mused, as she climbed back on the bank. She hung the tattered clothes to dry in the wind, and naked she collected firewood, as much as she could find. She assembled several layers of the thickest logs of driftwood and fallen trees at the bottom and stacked dozens of branches over the logs. On top of that, she placed an armful of sticks and tinder wood.

Confidently, she grabbed a handful of bark and started channelling heat through her hands. Devoid of nearby fires, and without the shard to enhance her abilities, she focused her attention until the smoke emerged from between her fingers. Around her, the wind grew cold and strong as Ada sucked the heat out of the air. Once the wood caught fire, the wind helped it spread. Soon, Ada stood naked in front of a pyre at tall as herself, the flames twice as high.

She let it burn for a while until she placed the dog on top and watched the fire consume it.

Afterwards, she went back to Rayn. The river had washed away the grime, and what remained of her clothes did not conceal what the rats had done to her. Ada winced.

'I'm sorry, my dear friend.'

With considerable effort, she managed to drag, lift and push Rayn on to the pyre. She stood still, staring as the flames finished the job the rats had started.

When only charred bones remained, she waded back into the river to drink and wash away the soot and smell from the fire. She brought her clothes over to the south bank of the river, and let the wind dry her skin before she put them on. Her clothes were not yet dry, but walking in the midday sun would remedy that.

'Thank you,' she said.

'I promised I would send for you,' the wind replied.

'I never doubted you. What do you need me to do?'

'You have to go back to the city and find the two shards in the old castle,' it said.

'Why?' The thought of returning to Sha'ton did not appeal to her.

'Because the demon who inhabits the castle will be able to cause much harm with the shards in his possession.'

'A demon?' Ada exclaimed. 'What is a demon? What does it look like, and what do I do if I find it?'

'You will see when you get there. You will find a way. Now, go! Before it kills again.'

Chapter 48: Flags

'The stadium manager has invented a new game. It's called "Catch the flag", and you guys are making history,' Zekatar said, looking at his gladiators.

Hobble followed the dark elf's gaze and looked around. They were gathered in one of the 'waiting rooms' under the stadium. Of course, it was more of a cell than a room, but at least they were not locked in. Besides Hobble and Zekatar, there were four others in the room. Two large humans called Bjorn and Bjarn, a dwarf named Craion and a female half-elf calling herself Queen. Bjorn and Bjarn were twins, muscular, blond and fair-skinned. Their bare torsos covered in dark tattoos. Craion was the prototypical dwarf. Red bearded and carrying an axe and a shield. Queen sat on a barrel looking uninterested. She wore black leather armour and dozens of knives.

'You'll face another team of five. And you'll have three flags on your side of the ground. You are the red team, and you will have red flags,' the dark elf said, and held up red ribbons. 'The other team will have three blue flags. Your job is to defend the red flags while at the same time capture the blue flags. Once you have one of the blue flags, you will have to carry it over to your side and mount it next to one of your red ones. Once this is done, you'll have one point. First to three points win.'

'Are there any other rules?' the dwarf Craion asked.

'Not that I am aware of,' Zekatar replied.

'So I can decapitate the blue team and then appropriate all the flags?'

'I guess you can,' Zekatar said, 'but I doubt that will be the best tactic. Remember this is a new game, and the team that adapts fastest is the team that will win. And as you know so well, I do not much enjoy losing.'

Zekatar took Hobble by the arm and led him a few paces away. 'Between you and me—it would be good if this match lasted a while.'

Hobble gave the dark elf a questioning look.

'Good for what comes later this night, I mean.' With that, Zekatar left the room.

Hobble did not know what to make of that information, but seeing the other gladiators looking at him, he pushed the thought to the back of his mind. He walked over to the others. 'So, what's the plan?'

'Without being privileged to all relevant information,' the dwarf said in a nasal voice, 'I propose a strategy where we distribute our métiers deliberately and meticulously.'

The twins looked at each other and shrugged. Queen rolled her eyes and shook her head.

'Do you perhaps have a tangible suggestion, master dwarf?' Hobble said. 'And please use informal language, I am of the little people and don't much like big words.'

'Of course, sir. One should always strive to convey information in a distinct and comprehensible manner.'

'Small words, Craion, small.'

'Yes, sure. My suggestion … eh idea … is that we deploy … I mean set up … so that I stay at our middle flag, Bjarn on one side and Bjorn on the flag at the opposite side. That way we have strong defenders on each flank, and we can assist each other if need be. Our two stealthy comrades will be our attackers and runners. This way I think we'll have a reasonable chance of winning this game of catch the flag, which of course should've been called "capture the flag".'

Once more, the other gladiators looked at each other. It seemed that no one found anything lacking with the plan, and soon voiced their agreement.

The plan was set. All that remained was to wait.

*

The game was on. The red team had found their positions as suggested by Craion. The ground was littered with objects and obstacles. Torches and braziers lit up the field. The flags were spread out with about thirty feet between them. As soon as the start horn had sounded, Hobble crept behind a wheelbarrow laying on its side. From there he had moved to a huge log. The blue team was a group of orcs, practically ensuring that the match would be a bloody one. Two of the brutes had already passed Hobble on the way forward. On the right flank, Queen was stalking forward. Hobble glanced around the end of the log. At the far wall, he could see one of the orcs standing by the leftmost blue flag. Creeping forward, he kept to the shadows and moved towards the left.

A cry from behind followed by a roar from the audience told Hobble that the fight was on. He willed the shadows to engulf him and quickened his pace. Soon, he closed in at the blue flag to the left and the orc guarding it. The orc stood looking around and slapping the head of a giant axe in his palm. Hobble envisaged being hit with that axe, and a shudder went through him. A moderately good hit would cleave him. From head to hairy foot. He could not risk an open fight with the brute.

An explosion of movement on the right flank made the guard in front of Hobble turn his head and take a step in that direction. That was all Hobble needed. Coming out in the torchlight a few feet from the flag, he would reach it before the orc could do anything about it. He did. However, at the same moment he got his hands on the flag, a few thousand spectators in the stands realised what was happening. The orc turned around. The hunt was on.

Hobble headed towards the red side of the ground and ran for the nearest obstacle. Coming to a cart, he slid under. Knowing that the cart would not slow the orc much, Hobble chose to change direction while in cover. He came out running to the right flank where Queen had made her move. The orc jumped over the cart before he realised what the halfling was up to. The orc growled while Hobble ran for the next obstacle, a stack of barrels. It was too far. Hobble could hear the orc gaining on him with every step. The halfling slid behind the barrels and scrambled for the shadows. Drawing on his magic, he hoped it was enough to cover him. The brute came around the barrels and looked around. Not finding what he was looking for, he sniffed the air. Hobble followed the path of shadows and did not look back.

A hush went through the spectators as they too lost sight of the halfling. Hobble crept through the shadows for a few moments more. Then he ran. Not looking back, barely glancing to the side he ran for his life. Bjarn took a step forward, cheering him on and securing Hobble's flag run. The halfling climbed the mount and fastened the blue flag next to the red. They were one point up.

After the early lead, the match became messy. Queen scored a flag run, but the orcs came back. Chasing in a single pack, they secured two flags and stopped Queen from completing her second run in the same process. In a few moments, the tide had turned. The score was two against two, but the orcs had all the momentum. Queen was down and out, and both Bjorn and Bjarn were bleeding badly. The only chance the red team had, was to secure a quick victory. Both teams had just one flag to defend, which made the match more straightforward.

'We push against their flag together,' Craion said, while both teams regrouped. When the brutes are deep into the battle, you go for their flag, Hobble.'

'Fair enough,' Hobble replied.

Bjarn and Bjorn leaned on their heavy weapons, breathing.

'Ready?' The dwarf asked.

'The sooner,' Bjarn started.

'The better,' Bjorn finished.

Craion led the charge, shouting a battle cry that Hobble did not understand. Hobble followed the twins holding tight to his staff while he ran as fast as his limping allowed him. The orcs did not shy from an open fight and came to meet them in the centre of the ground. The spectators clearly appreciated the less than subtle approach and took their cheering to new heights.

Over the next quarter, the game was more a fight than a game of catching the flags. Hobble continued to weave in and out on the different targets. Swinging his staff here, dodging an axe there, all the way looking for an opening to slip away.

*

Hobble had found his opening. While the orc was consumed by the battle, he had slipped away, caught the last blue flag and found his way across the field.

Closing in on his goal, Hobble heard running feet behind him. He glanced over his shoulder and saw an orc in full pursuit. The flag mount was thirty feet away. He had to make it. A loud murmur rose as the spectators understood what was going on. The orc came closer for every step, every inch. Hobble considered calling for the wind, but had no idea how to use it to increase his pace. No, it had to go, he was so close. Closing in on the mount, he lifted the flag. Behind him, the orc growled. Hobble jumped. Raised the flag.

And slotted it home!

Hobble fell. He turned as the orc skidded to a stop above him. The brute had his axe lifted and ready to strike. His eyes were large, his brow knitted and his nostrils flaring. A growl escaped from his snarling mouth. Saliva dripped. Hobble closed his eyes.

A voice boomed over the stadium. 'Stop! Lay down your weapons! Red team wins!'

Hobble opened one eye. The brute above held the same pose. The same feral expression. His muscles were shaking. The internal struggle plain to see in the orc's eyes. He wanted nothing more than to plant his axe in the helpless halfling laying before him. Hobble raised a hand in front of himself, and started shuffling back and away. Inch by inch, he drew away, and at last, he could breathe again.

The orc relaxed. Straightening, he brought his weapon down to his side.

The match was won. Hobble was still alive.

The real fight yet to come.

Chapter 49: Throne room

Gilmir stepped into what undoubtedly was the throne room. The contrast to the city, in general, was stunning. The servants' entrance he came through was behind heavy red curtains hanging from the marble ceiling high above. Around him, green plants rose from huge vases, and a massive pillar of black stone stood to his left. A few steps in front of him and to the right, majestic stairs led up to a dais.

The spacious room seemed to be empty, if no one was hiding or standing on the part of the podium he could not yet see. Stalking forward he came in full view of the dominating feature of the room. On each side of the stairs, there were gilded statues of some strange humanoid shapes riding creatures best described as winged toads. Their eyes and other features were outlined with green stones. Possibly emeralds or something resembling.

Up the stairs, the dais came in view. On each side of the platform, curving stairs led to a second dais supporting a tremendous canopied throne. However, the throne was not what caught your eye when standing in front of the stairs. The most stunning feature of the room was the giant windows behind the high seat. Spanning the entire length of two corner walls, the windows revealed a breathtaking view of the city of Shacktown. This was the throne room of a king.

Drawn to the windows, Gilmir started up the stairs. On the first dais, he saw display cases circling the foot of the throne. He felt the shards before he saw them. Resonating with the one he carried in a pouch around his neck, the power virtually crackled. Gingerly he stepped closer. Three thumb-sized shards were displayed in three separate compartments. The urge to pick up the stones tugged at his soul. Knowing it would be a fatal mistake, he turned his attention to the case to the right of the ones occupied with stones. This one displayed two swords. One long blade lying beside its scabbard and the shorter blade in its sheath.

These were his swords. *Megil an* and *Megil ai*. The single-edged, slightly curved swords did not look like anything out of the ordinary. With worn grips and narrow blades, they seemed almost out of sort next to the shards and other artefacts on display. However, made of jewel steel, in a process taking three master swordsmiths and dozens of assistants several months, these elven blades were the most precious artefacts Gilmir had ever owned. The fact was that he would trade his magic shard for the blades in an instant. Opening the display case, he gently picked up his blades.

Sliding the shorter blade from the scabbard, he lifted the swords in front of him. It was like reuniting with an old friend, a brother, a part of himself. The elf smiled, cutting the air and swirling around, making strikes and thrusts. Feeling like a child emulating the great warriors on the swordsman terrace, he fell into an old and trusted routine. The pattern of strikes, parries and thrusts he had been doing daily for most of his life. The world came to order, the stars aligned, his soul centred. He had found himself, he was back, he was home. Whole.

'By all means make yourself at home,' a voice said behind him. Consumed by his sword dance, Gilmir had not noticed anyone approaching. However, he knew that voice. This was the man who had tortured him for hours, days, weeks. This man had drowned him, burned him, pulled fingernails off him. This man had nearly broken him. It had been so close that Gilmir remembered deciding he would tell the man everything he wanted to know. That he would do anything to make him stop. Except, before he managed to let the man know this, he had been back in his cell never to revisit the torture chamber.

Had Gilmir not been holding his blades, had he not felt the worn, comforting leather of the hilts against his palms, had he not just at that moment been deep into the meditating sword dance, he would have broken right there. On the dais in front of the throne. Before ever facing the man. However, he was centred, calm and collected. He took a deep breath and turned.

In front of the stairs stood Voan. Tall and broad-shouldered, with dark hair falling down to his shoulders. A bandana of some sort covered his mouth and nose. A black silk shirt and white linen trousers were visible under a dark red cloak reaching the floor. He covered his right hand inside the opening of his shirt, making it look like it was hurt. At his hip, he bore a long sword. Voan pulled down the bandana revealing a casual smile. Looking at that smile, Gilmir knew he had been betrayed. Four guards carrying halberds flanked the man, while another two stood in front of the massive double doors. Between the guards in the back and the ones surrounding Voan, stood a robed figure, a priest of some sort. He carried a pot with burning incense hanging from fine chains.

'I do believe these are mine,' Gilmir said, lifting his swords.

'Are you certain?' Voan said. 'Those blades belonged to an assassin and spy I caught and sentenced to life in prison a few years ago. If you are the owner of those blades, you give me no choice but to have my guards arrest you again.'

'Whatever happens here, serpent, I can assure you that I will not be going back to that hole you call a prison,' Gilmir said, studying the man's face for any reaction to his choice of words.

Revealing nothing, Voan replied calmly. 'That is a shame, I was hoping we could continue our little game on the stone table you know so well. I think a taste of freedom was exactly what you needed to reignite that spirit of yours. Making torturing you all the more fun. Not to speak of the fact that it would make it easier to break you. It was actually recommended in a fascinating old book on torture from the Elfwar. Letting prisoners escape or think they would escape, giving them false hope, and then recapturing them. My advisors said it would be risky. I knew you would come back. By your own volition.'

Gilmir opened his mouth, but no words came out.

'Surprised, are we? Did you think the halfling came sauntering by your cell that day by coincidence?'

'I will kill you,' Gilmir said through gritted teeth, 'Even if it is the last thing I do, I will end your life and make this world a better place in the process.' With that, he lifted his blades and crouched.

'Big words from a puny soul. You are not worth my time, elf,' Voan replied, before he beckoned his guards forward, 'Take him out, boys!'

Waiting at the top of the stairs, Gilmir prepared for the fight of his life. The two first guards came side by side up the stairs, their halberds pointing forward. They were in no rush, and soon the two other guards flanked them. Gilmir backed up and to the side, finding one of the narrower stairs. He continued retreating, knowing that they would have to come one and one to reach him there. As soon as the guards reached the plateau, two of them ran towards the other stairs. In a few beats, they would reach him from the other side. Gilmir was out of time.

'Oh, come on, boys! He is one feeble elf. Get him, already!'

One of the guards heeded the command and came forward, thrusting his halberd. It was a simple and straightforward attack. Gilmir batted the weapon away with his short blade and followed up with a swing with the other sword towards the man's head. The guard had to back off and nearly tangled with his companion coming behind. Anticipating this, Gilmir took two quick steps forward and plunged his short sword into the man's stomach. The second guard stabbed his halberd. Gilmir whipped his long blade across, cutting clean through the halberd shaft. The guard's eyes widened, and he stumbled backwards. Coming down the curving stairs Gilmir slid on his knees over the stone tiled floor towards the man. Both blades whipping across in front of him and hitting the outside of the man's leading foot above his knee. The larger blade went straight through, toppling the guard helpless on the floor. Gilmir came to his feet and looked around.

The two guards on the top dais stopped by the throne, obviously unsure how to proceed. Voan still stood in front of the stairs. His calm smile had vanished, replaced by a scowl. The two guards by the door had taken a few steps into the room. Two more guards came into view from behind the curtains on either side of the stairs.

'Take him!' Voan roared.

Chapter 50: Dance

Hobble heard fighting and shouting from the open doors. Keeping close to the wall, he stalked forward. He reached the opening and peered through. Two guards stood with their backs to him a few steps into the room. Further in, a robed figure stood gently swinging a pot of incense. The room smelled of that incense, lavender and pipe tobacco. In front of a broad stair leading to the throne dais, Voan stood with a sword in his left hand. However, it was the spectacle in front of the panorama windows that drew Hobble's gaze.

Gilmir fought two guards, and it took Hobble's breath away. The economy of movement the elf displayed was spectacular. He moved like running water. Like a breeze through the trees. He was not fighting, he was dancing.

One of the guards stabbed at Gilmir with the spear point of the halberd. The other guard chopped with the axe part of the weapon. The two attacks were well coordinated and flawlessly executed. Gilmir avoided the spear-thrust with the slightest of movements. Turning his body, the weapon missed him by an inch. With his short blade, he deflected the axe blow in the direction of the other halberd, tangling the two weapons in the process. With his curved sword, he slashed. The weapon cut across the man's face. In the next instance, the elf took a step forward and stabbed his short blade, impaling the other man in the stomach. The two guards fell to the floor, clutching their wounds, ending the fight within beats.

Hobble shook his head, realising he had to move if he was to do something about this. Creeping forward he closed in on the guard to the right. With an overhead chop of his staff, he hit the man over the head. The guard moaned and sank to the floor. Before the other guard could turn, Hobble moved again. Swinging the staff, he hit the other guard on the outside of the knee. The man buckled. But before he could do much more, Hobble had reversed momentum on his weapon bringing the other end crashing down on the man's head.

Glancing up, he saw Voan climbing the stairs towards Gilmir who stood by the throne waiting. The robed figure also moved forward, climbing the stairs. However, Hobble had more immediate concerns. Two guards came forward from the wall on each side of the stairs, which Hobble had not noticed. The men came towards Hobble, spear points leading. The halfling sighed. Ambushing and taking out two guards who did not know he existed was one thing, fighting two guards in a fair fight was something else entirely.

Chapter 51: Stunning

Ada needed no directions to find her way towards the top of the ancient castle. The power pulsating from above made it as clearly visible as any lighthouse. On her way there, she had passed dozens of servants and a handful of perfumed men and women wearing silk and jewellery. She spotted a couple of guards as well, but nobody made any attempt at stopping her.

Before she reached the double doors, the ringing clang of steel against steel, and the grunting and screams of fighting men, greeted her.

I'm too late.

Ada turned the corner and entered the room. She stopped briefly to take in the scene. The throne room was stunning. Daylight entering through the huge windows behind the elevated throne reflected on the marble surfaces and golden statues. Multiple curtains created contrasting shadows, and the smell of lavender and incense hung heavy in the air.

The breathtaking scene was, however, marred by the sounds and images of a melee.

Among the combatants were two familiar figures, her companions from the fight against the undead in the graveyard the night they entered the city. To her left, Hobble was using his staff to keep two guards at bay and avoid getting skewered on their long halberds. Next to the throne, his silhouette dramatically outlined against the windows behind him, Gilmir was holding curved swords, eyeing his opponent at the bottom of the stairs. A handful of guards lay dead or severely wounded on the floor.

A broad-shouldered man in a red cloak sauntered towards the elf, a long sword in hand. His posture and deliberate movements radiated confidence, even superiority, as he approached his foe.

In the chaos, Ada's attention was drawn to the robed man picking up a starglass from a display case on the plateau between the two flights of stairs. The familiar hum filled the room, revealing to Ada the immediate presence of other shards. The man bent to his knees next to a prone guard. With the trained hands of an expert healer, he quickly examined the guard's wounds, breathing and pulse. Beats later, he nodded and started speaking in a low voice. The ceremonial litany of a cleric, Ada assumed.

Kneeling, the cleric reached inside his robe and produced a knife. Without hesitation, he pushed the blade down on the left side of the guard's neck, in the soft area just above the collarbone. Still uttering his recital, he twisted the knife a few times, before he pulled it out and put it on the floor in front of him, next to the shard.

Ada watched, unable to comprehend what the cleric was trying to achieve. The answer struck her like the blow from a hammer when the robed man picked up the shard and inserted it fully into the wound he had made with his knife.

'No!' Ada screamed and ran towards the cleric and the prone guard.

Alerted by her scream, the cleric turned to look at her. As his gaze met her, thunder erupted inside Ada's mind. There was no sound, but waves of thunder, nonetheless. Unable to focus or coordinate the most basic of movements, she lost control of her feet mid-stride and fell face first on the marble floor.

Stunned, she could only watch as the dead guard rose and picked up his halberd.

Chapter 52: Voan

Gilmir stood by the throne on the top dais watching Voan calmly climbing the curving stairs. The imposing man was in no rush. Further down, the robed man ascended the first stairs. Gilmir looked around on the plateau. Behind the throne, a giant battleaxe rested against the back of the chair. On a small table by the high seat, there were candles smelling of lavender, bottles of liquids, jars containing salves and more incense. Below the stairs, Hobble had arrived and was fighting two guards. By the doors, a servant girl stood staring at the carnage. The robed man collected a shard from the display cases causing a new pitch to the melody between the stones.

Voan was near the top. The robed man clutched the stone and knelt by one of the dead guards. Healing or necromancy? Identifying the resonance from the man's shard, Gilmir knew the answer. He shifted his attention to Voan, who climbed the last steps now. The man had covered the lower part of his face with the bandana again, hiding any facial expression.

'A necromancer?' Gilmir asked while stepping behind the throne and facing Voan on the walkway. 'You have a necromancer in your ranks?'

'Oh, why not, elf? Magic is magic. It's all the same. Energy,' Voan said, cutting the air with his sword. He shrugged off his cloak, his right hand inside the shirt. Something was odd with that hand—that arm. It was huge. Now that the cloak did not hide it, the proportions became clear. Gilmir wondered what was wrong with it.

'Let's get this over with.' Voan stepped closer on the ledge behind the throne.

Voan swung his longsword, leading with his left foot he took up a position similar to a fencer with a much lighter weapon. With such a pose, the man would not get too much force behind his strikes. However, he could put his considerable weight behind the stabs and lunges. Parrying the first strike had the elf doubting his reasoning. Unnatural strength drove that swing. Even with his deft deflection, redirecting most of the force, Gilmir felt the impact jolting up his arm. He would have to go for speed.

Voan came on, slashing and stabbing. Gilmir backed away while he dodged and parried. Soon he would be at the end of the plateau, backed up against the descending stairs. The fighting started to take its toll. A few days ago, he was dying in a cell. The convalescence had been quick and thorough, but he was nowhere near his best shape. Unfortunately, he probably had to be, to defeat this opponent and live through the day.

Gilmir glanced over his shoulder. Voan did not hesitate. A quick step forward, and he lunged. With his long blade, Gilmir parried and drove the longsword to the side. He took advantage of the momentum and pivoted, coming around with his short sword slashing against Voan's exposed neck. With his longsword out wide, he was unable to parry the strike. Gilmir had him.

Or so he thought. Voan's right hand came out from the fold of his shirt. The giant limb caught Gilmir's blade in a tight grip. Scales covered the back of the hand, the skin shining with a hint of green. In this position, they froze for a moment. Gilmir remembered the reptile smell from the man back in the torture chamber. He could see the grin on Voan's face just by looking at his eyes.

With a tight grip on the blade, Voan wrenched it out of Gilmir's hand. Taking a step back, he dropped it over the ledge. The sword clanged down by the foot of the throne, on the lower platform. 'It's a bit unfair that you have two blades and I only have one.'

Glad for the pause, Gilmir took the moment to centre himself. Focusing on his breath he did not respond.

Voan glanced down on his monstrous right hand while he continued stepping backwards. 'It is a fine pair of blades you have, elf. I'll give you that. Usually, I can do that without a scratch on my hand. Your little sword cut me. But do not worry, my friend, it is just a scratch.' He placed the longsword in the palm and closed his eyes. Drawing the sword over his hand, a green light danced along the edge of the blade. He was casting a spell.

Gilmir exploded forward, hoping to get a jump on the man. In the last instance, the man opened his eyes and parried the blow. Turning the blade, he hit back with his monstrous fist. Turning and dodging, Gilmir avoided the blow. He stepped back, centring his balance and raising his blade again. This time Voan came forward. Anticipating Gilmir's back-pedalling, he stepped forward, stabbing. This time, Gilmir could not step away. He turned, but too late.

The sword plunged into skin and flesh. Gilmir gasped.

Chapter 53: Circling

Hobble circled to avoid being flanked by the two approaching guards. Realising he would be hard-pressed to defeat the two guards, he focused his mind. Reaching out for the currents of air, he tried collecting them. Tried to mould them, focusing them, gathering them in a sharp torrent. However, in this room atop the castle, there was not much movement in the air. Hardly any wind energy at all.

The first guard stabbed at him. Hobble batted the weapon away, and stepped back to avoid the expected chop from the other guard. Circling, he waited for the right moment. The guards worked well together, stabbing and chopping, chopping and stabbing, and not leaving any room for him to counter.

Hobble noticed that another person had entered the room and seemed to be fighting the robed man and a guard. However much he wanted to look over and establish who this person was, he did not dare take his eyes away from the two guards.

Chapter 54: Sleep

As the numbing effect of the thunder waves decreased with every heartbeat, Ada lay still on the marble floor and let her eyes explore the throne room. She took it all in, absorbing every relevant piece of information. At the uppermost dais, next to the throne, the elf and the red-cloaked man engaged in a duel of words and insults. The way they shifted their feet and flicked their swords in preparation indicated that there would soon be a furious duel between two expert swordsmen.

The ongoing fight between the halfling and the two guards seemed to be balanced. The guards had a larger reach with their halberds, but the quicker halfling kept moving around in circles to prevent his two opponents from splitting up and flanking him.

That left Ada to contend with the cleric and the undead guard that walked towards her, with the halberd raised for a devastating chop.

Ada forced herself to remain still for a few beats longer until the undead stopped right in front of her. As the lower part of the elongated shaft of the halberd moved into her field of vision, she rolled to the right. Her muscles were slow and weakened, and a living man would have been able to adjust the arc of the swing and land the axe blade in her back. The undead, slowed by the unnatural state of its entire being, could not. The halberd crashed into the polished floor where Ada had laid a moment earlier, spreading sparks and pieces of marble in every direction.

Driven by fear and necessity, Ada sprang to her feet and barely evaded a horizontal backhand swing with the halberd. The ten-foot polearm was the perfect weapon for the undead, as the unsurpassed reach and heavy damage potential compensated for the slowness of its wielder. One hit would be enough to finish the battle, and anyone trying to dodge those deadly swings would soon tire.

Ada considered running straight at the cleric but decided against it when she took into account how easily he had incapacitated her with his stun spell. If he managed to immobilise her again, only for a beat, the undead would split her in half as she stood.

Instead, she ran to the outer perimeters of the room, using the statues, curtains and decorations to limit the undead's movements and the effectiveness of the halberd's swings. Several times, the weapon got stuck in wood or fabric, and in the brief respites, Ada saw that the halfling was still fighting the two guards. It seemed to Ada that he was gaining the upper hand. If she could stay alive long enough for him to finish the two, he would be able to help her.

The surge of optimism was short-lived.

Ada was not far from the double doors through which she had entered the throne room. The undead had been chopping its way along the walls, after her. Statues were tilted, curtains pulled down, and there was little left standing to use for cover on this side of the room. Just as she prepared to dash across the open floor to the other side, she was overtaken by fatigue. She could feel her mind and body shutting down, about to fall asleep.

'Your mind is wide open! Protect yourself!' the wind said, inside her head.

The command jolted her, enough to roll away from another swing.

'Fight back!' it said.

Ada did not understand what the voice meant. Too exhausted to fight, or even to move, she slumped to the floor, perfectly at ease. All she needed—all she ever wanted—was sleep, and in a few beats, she would be sleeping.

'You better not!' a deep voice barked.

Above, she heard the crash of wood impacting on wood, followed by the noise of dozens of items breaking against the floor.

Ada opened her eyes to see a dwarf entangled with the undead guard among a heap of broken wood and ceramics less than ten feet away from her. She briefly pondered what the dwarf was doing here, but soon concluded that she did not care.

'He's doing this to you! Fight him!' the wind said.

'How?' she whispered.

'Any way you can.'

Chapter 55: Shatter

Backing away, Gilmir examined the wound with his free hand. Blood was already gathering on the left side of his stomach. A flesh wound. But not just a flesh wound. Gilmir felt the taint of foul magic. Felt his life force leaking out with the blood. A glance at Voan confirmed his fear. The crinkling of the skin around the man's eyes revealed a grin.

'Don't worry, friend. It's just a flesh wound. Nothing to worry about for a great elven warrior.'

Gilmir fell on one knee, holding his hand on the wound and grimacing.

'What?' Voan said, taking a few steps towards the elf. 'Was that all? A small gash and the exceptional warrior falls to his knees. I had expected more from an elf of the finest lineage.'

Gilmir closed his eyes. Hearing the man moving forward, sensing the foul energy of the magic sword. He sensed the weapon coming forward in a rush and drew on the energy of the shard around his neck. Directing the force to his muscles, he burst into movement. He opened his eyes and slashed the long blade towards the stabbing sword. Going for the hilt and the hand holding it, he scored a hit. Voan dropped the sword. It too fell over the ledge and down to the platform below. Gilmir got to his feet and pressed the advance. The blade coming the other way striking at the man's torso. Voan jumped back, narrowly avoiding the attack. Gilmir kept coming forward, kept striking. Falling into attacking routines practised to perfection over a human lifetime. Voan dodged and retreated, somehow managing to avoid being hit. Building momentum Gilmir went for a desperate finish. He slid down on his knees. He came in low and made it hard for his adversary to retreat. The blade slashed out, cutting a gash in Voan's thigh.

Voan growled. Gilmir's momentum stopped. Ignoring the wound, Voan moved out of reach, picking up the battleaxe behind the throne in the process.

'You are starting to annoy me, elf!' Voan said, swinging the colossal battleaxe with his right hand.

Gilmir glanced to the left, to the small table by the throne. Nodding towards the flasks, pots and incense. 'How have you been feeling lately?'

'What the hell are you talking about?'

'The face mask, the lavender, the elven tobacco, the ointments and creams, those won't help you,' Gilmir said, holding one hand at his wound and the blade pointing at the man.

'What are you playing at, elf? I don't take health advice from an assassin!'

'Sound logic. Thus, I wonder why you would consult with a necromancer?' Gilmir tilted his head towards the robed figure below. 'Don't you realise he is the one making you sick? He's poisoning you and making himself invaluable by remedying his own poisons.'

Voan eyes widened ever so slightly before he cast a glance down into the room. Gilmir came forward. He fell into a vicious attacking routine. A sequence of swings and thrusts made for one outcome. Building up for a killing blow and foregoing all defence in the process. Voan brought his huge axe up to parry. Once, twice, three times. He stepped back, dodged and twisted. With his momentum building, Gilmir was close to the grand finale. Taking a step forward, he gripped the sword with two hands and slashed. It would have been the killing blow if it had reached its target. Instead, a boot in his gut sent him backwards. Voan followed and sent the axe in a mighty sidelong chop against Gilmir's head. The elf sensed the weapon touching his hairs as he fell backwards. The heavy axe crashed into one of the great windows, shattering it.

Wind gushed in. The setting sun reflected in one of the golden window frames. Gilmir lay on his back. Voan took a step forward, his axe was once again ready to strike. The wound in Gilmir's stomach throbbed and weakened him. He had nowhere to move, no way to resist the massive axe descending on him.

Chapter 56: Wind

Hobble dodged, parried, jumped and backed away. He had scored a few jabs to the body of one of the guards, but most of the time he was forced to defend. The two guards fought well together, and were probably trained for that purpose. Hobble was losing. His feet were tiring. His arms felt heavy. The guards knew it too. A smile spread across the face of the taller of them.

'Follow my lead,' the tall man said, 'We got this little rat now!'

A chopping halberd came down at Hobble. He jumped backwards. The other guard followed up, moving forward and stabbing. The halfling stepped aside. Another stab. Hobble parried. When the third stab came, he was out of balance. Falling to his knees was the only option he saw. The first guard stepped in, his halberd up high again. The axe part came rushing down. Hobble had nowhere to go. He tried desperately to bring his staff to bear.

A crash sounded.

Hobble could feel the energy building in an instance. Not thinking, just reacting, he gathered the moving air, channelled it and sent it through his silver oak staff. The staff flew out batting the halberd away and out of the guard's hands. Reversing momentum, he swung the other end into the outside of the man's knee. Feeling it shatter, the halfling got to his feet and let the other end of the staff crash into the helpless man's face. From there, the staff shot straight right, connecting with the other guard's head. Once again reversing momentum, Hobble spun the weapon over his head. The other end crashed into the man's head from the opposite side.

Lifting his gaze, Hobble realised that although he had won the fight, the battle was far from over.

Chapter 57: Choke

A loud crash followed by a cold gust of wind woke Ada up.

Next to her, a dwarf she had never seen before swung a battleaxe against the undead guardsman, landing blow after blow. Nevertheless, he was losing the fight, as wounds that would have killed a man failed to have the same effect on a man already dead. To make things worse, the axe blade sometimes got stuck following the hardest blows, and it was no easy feat for the dwarf to wiggle it loose before the halberd struck him.

Ada got to her feet, ran towards the pair and leapt on the undead's back. The impact forced it to take a step forward to keep its balance and denied it the chance to swing at the dwarf.

'Thanks, lass,' the dwarf grunted.

Ada flung her arms around the undead's head, covering its eyes. She did not know if it needed eyes to see, or whether it could keep fighting unhampered without. But it seemed bothered enough to use one hand to pull Ada off, leaving only one hand to hold the halberd.

The dwarf seized the opportunity to swing at the halberd shaft, an inch or two from the hand that held it. The blow sent the polearm flying across the room, leaving the undead guardsman without a weapon.

A shout in an unfamiliar language made Ada turn her head towards the cleric. Standing in the middle of the room, he pointed at the dwarf with the index and middle finger of his right hand, reciting some spell or curse.

At that moment, the undead got hold of Ada's upper arm and pulled her off its back in an overhead arc. The air knocked out of her as she slammed to the floor. Before she could move, the undead bent over her, trying to choke her.

Ada fought desperately to keep the sticky fingers from closing around her neck, but he was far too strong for her. All she could do was grab hold of his thumbs with each hand, and to some extent divert the pressure on her windpipe. It would take her a bit longer to die, but she would undoubtedly die.

Closing her eyes, she reached out and connected with the shard inserted in the undead guardsman. The shard vibrated with power, humming menacingly like a hive of wasps. Ada fuelled it with the energy of her own fear and desperation, magnifying the intensity and pitch. She released every emotion from her time in the dungeon cell. Her grief over Rayn's death, the horror of the rats, the hunger, the desire to live. She opened her eyes, stared straight into the dead eyes of the guardsman, and channelled the insuppressible urge to breathe.

The shard's pitch increased even further until no longer audible. It was silent for a while, and the only sound Ada heard was the heavy beat of her own heart. The room went dark for an instant.

Then, the shard released its energy, shattering inside the undead guard. The room flashed brightly.

The heavy corpse, killed twice in quick succession, fell over Ada.

Chapter 58: Light

The sunlight in the window's frame, the daylight in the room, the particles of colour and light around him. All of this Gilmir gathered, collected, assembled into his soul. In a reversed flash, his surroundings became dark. Like from a lightning bolt of darkness. He pointed his left hand in front of him. Directing it towards Voan. Aiming.

Then he released. All the light, the sun rays, the colour, the energy, freed. It shot out of his hand, hitting the devil spawn in front of him in the face and leaving the rest of the room in shadows. Not for long.

For the span of a lightning strike. For a fraction of a heartbeat.

The room settled in its normal light again.

Voan, although blinded, was not hurt. Reacting fast, he let his axe fall. Ending the elf.

But Gilmir was not there anymore.

Standing behind the monstrous man, he stabbed his long blade into the small of Voan's back and drove it in and up. Letting the curved blade find its natural way through flesh, bones and vital organs, he whispered in the dying man's ear.

'Never turn your back to an assassin.'

Chapter 59: Fits

Ada turned her head to look for the dwarf who had come to her rescue.

She found him on the floor five feet away from her, shaking violently.

'Fits!' she said, and pushed the guard off from her.

As she rose, she drew a dagger from his belt and walked straight towards the evil cleric. To her left, the halfling stood leaning on his staff. By the throne above, the elf pulled his curved blade out of the back of his prone opponent.

Ada recognised the silent thunder that had left her incapacitated in the first attack. This time, the cleric's desperate efforts were nothing more than a nuisance. She was beyond him, and the frightened man held no power over her.

She stopped right in front of him, dagger in hand.

'Look around. They're all dead. You've lost,' she said.

To his credit, the cleric did glance around. He did not utter a word, but his eyes said it all.

'Take off your robe,' she commanded.

After a moment's hesitation, he obeyed and let the black robe fall to the floor. Underneath, he wore ordinary wool clothing, suitable for the season. Ada resisted the temptation to take them as well.

'Leave, before I change my mind,' she said.

The cleric nodded and ran for the doors.

Ada quickly pulled the robes over her head, and returned to examine the dwarf. His whole body was convulsing, his mouth foamed and his pants were soiled. 'Who is he?'

'Tracks,' Hobble answered.

'Friend of yours?'

'After today, yes. What's happening to him?'

'He's got the fits. I think the cleric cursed him during the fight.'

'Can you do something?'

'I don't think so,' Ada said.

'This should help,' Gilmir said, as he came down the stairs. In his hand, he held a vial containing a milky liquid, which he had uncorked. He held it under his nose and sniffed. As he joined them, he put a finger on top and turned the vial upside down for a beat. He licked his finger and made a show of tasting the sample from the vial.

'What is it?' Hobble said.

'Dormicus, I believe,' Gilmir said

'What's that?'

'Sedative. Tranquiliser. Useful for inducing sleep, and for situations like these.' Gilmir pointed at the dwarf.

'Well, what are you waiting for? Give it to him!'

'That's the tricky part. In his state, he can't drink it. He's unconscious, so he wouldn't be able to swallow. He would choke on it.'

'You're quite useless, you know that? How do you suggest we give it to him, then?'

'Well, if the front door is locked, one would have to use the servant's entrance,' Gilmir said, with a sly smile.

Hobble stared at Gilmir. His face reddened, and he threw Ada a glance.

'It's an analogy.' This time the elf was grinning.

'The servant's … Absolutely not! Not gonna happen!'

'Alright, alright! There is another way,' Gilmir said, and handed the vial to Hobble. 'Smear this in his mouth, on the inside of his cheeks and lips.'

The halfling seemed unimpressed but accepted the task. Moments later, he was kneeling next to the dwarf's head, applying the contents of the vial. 'Like this?'

'Yes, just like that,' Gilmir said. 'But be careful …'

'Careful about what?'

The elf didn't reply.

'Balls!' Hobble shouted, and pulled his hand away from the dwarf.

'Be careful with your fingers. It's quite common to be bitten when you do that.' Gilmir grinned.

Chapter 60: King

Tracks responded well to the treatment. He soon sat, looking around the room and at himself.

'Musta been a damn good fight!' he grunted. 'It's been ages since I shat myself in battle.'

The sound of slow applause made all four of them turn towards the door.

Ada gasped as she recognised Zekatar.

'Well done, my champions!' Zekatar said. 'You've done a great deed today, ridding the city and the whole world of this half-demon.' His words were polite, but the smirk on his face made them worthless.

He entered the room and walked confidently up to them. A rapier hung by his hip, but if he felt threatened in their company, he did an excellent job of hiding it.

Stopping in front of Hobble, he reached out his hand, palm up. Waiting.

Hobble looked uncomfortable and glanced from Zekatar to Gilmir and back several times. Zekatar didn't move. The halfling shifted from foot to foot, obviously facing a dilemma of some sort.

Eventually, he seemed to lose a battle of will, reached into his pocket and produced a starglass. He put it in Zekatar's hand. Demonstrating his absolute command of the situation, the drow kept his hand open, inviting the halfling or anyone else to change the course of the transaction. Satisfied, he closed his hand around the shard and walked towards the dais.

'I am Zekatar', he said as he ascended the first stairs. 'Son of Sofodies, son of Zakari,' he continued, as he strolled up the second stairs. He paused at the shattered window, knowing he held everyone's attention. 'Rightful heir to the throne of Saiqtron.'

In front of the throne, he turned to face the four surviving combatants.

'Thank you, ladies and gentlefolk.' He sat down on the throne.

'Now, if you will all be so kind as to leave my throne room.'

Chapter 61: History

Gilmir and Hobble sat by the fireplace in a small room back in The Pick and the Axe. Chris had secured the private room for the four combatants as soon as they returned from the castle. Now she and Ada sat huddled together like old friends sharing tales after months apart. Gilmir felt sorry for Ada. The young girl had experienced more in the last day than most people lived through in years. By the door, Tracks stood shouting for more food and drinks. The unstable dwarf was in fine spirits and worked hard to ensure that his newfound friends had all they wanted. After taking a much-needed bath in a tub in the corner of the room, he had proclaimed his friendship to his brothers and sister in arms.

'One thing I don't understand,' Hobble said, forcing Gilmir's attention back to his little friend who was nursing a large mug of ale in both hands. 'How come there were no more guards comin'?

We must've been fightin' in that room for at least half an hour. Breaking furniture and smashin' windows. We had some real luck in the end.'

'Luck had nothing to do with it,' Gilmir answered, and swirled the wine in his glass.

'What do you mean?'

'Zekatar.'

'Stop with your bloody riddles, elf! Full sentences!'

'Zekatar had already initiated his coup before we entered the centre stage,' Gilmir said, smiling at the use of an analogy. 'He just needed us to do the hard part.'

'But how could he know? I didn't tell him nothin'!'

'He probably knew what was going on long before we did. He has been pulling the strings for a while.'

'What do you mean?'

'Victor and the men chasing you. Saendar and the information I got from him. Probably the spectacle leading to Ada and Rayn's imprisonment. Maybe more.'

'How do you know all this? Who *are* you?'

'A prince.' Gilmir did not miss a beat.

'Ha ha, no, you're not, but some kind of spy or assassin?' Hobble lowered his voice and looked around while ending the sentence.

'Let's just say that I have had some experience with these sorts of things: schemes and plots, coups and chaos.'

Hobble shook his head. 'Elves! You think you can go around manipulating innocents to be your sorry little game pieces. With no regard to how you are affecting the life of the innocents!'

'Yeah, you are not all wrong; however, I fail to find many innocent in this scheme. And speaking of innocent—and since we are asking questions …' Gilmir let the statement hang while he studied the halfling. Hobble looked up from his mug and wiped foam from his lips, looking like a boy caught with both hands in the cookie jar.

'I have thought about that night in the dungeons often. The night when you came parading by my cell …' Gilmir paused. Hobble looked down in his mug again. Looking for good answers where there were none. 'And the one thing I could not quite understand was how you could have your staff with you? I know the guards down there. All thirty-seven of them. And they would not allow a prisoner to keep a weapon, not even a staff. Which of course means that you were down there for some other reason? To free me? Why? Who sent you? Zekatar?'

'Yes. He was pulling the strings on that part, too.' Hobble lifted his gaze and met Gilmir's eyes, an apologetic look on his face.

'Did he tell you why?'

'No. The dark elf was never the sharing type.'

'But, you left me?' Gilmir followed up with another question.

'Yeah, I wasn't kiddin' when I said you would not make the swim. I didn't see how I could get you further at the time. In addition, I knew they lifted the bars occasionally and I figured you would find out if you did not die on the spot. Leaving you there, I reckoned you would not suspect foul play. Besides, Zekatar was not worried when I told him.' Hobble shrugged.

Gilmir pondered the answer, and decided he trusted the little thief. He chose not to comment on the whole lifting the bars situation and how he had not figured out that possibility. 'Because Zekatar knew about the hidden door.' Gilmir thought aloud.

'How do you reckon?'

'The information I got from Saendar. It was incredibly detailed. Although I don't doubt the knowledge and the mind of the old man, this was another level. As if it came from someone with intimate knowledge of the castle. Which leads me to another point. Did you hear Zekatar's proclamation as he ascended the stairs?'

'Yeah, some pompous statement. "I am Zekatar, son of whatshisname, son of whatshisname's father".'

'Something like that yeah. Except that Zakari—Zekatar's alleged grandfather—was the first king of Saiqtron.'

'Saiqtron?'

'The former dark elven city, now known as Shacktown.'

'Sha'ton was an elven city!?'

'Yes. And according to Zekatar, he is the heir to that throne. The rightful king of Saiqtron.'

'Whoa!'

'Exactly. This coup was probably about more than a councilman position.'

'And Ada?' Hobble asked. 'How come she was there? Was that also Zekatar's doing?'

'I don't know. I have to talk to her about that.' Gilmir turned his head, looking for the young woman. Ada was leaving the room, carrying a couple of empty mugs. Gilmir rose and followed.

Passing by the table where Chris and Tracks sat, Gilmir asked, 'Ada going for more drinks?'

'Yeah, she did not much like my whiskey,' Tracks replied. 'All the same, more for me!' The dwarf lifted two cups in a toast.

'And she would not let me go!' Chris said, laughing. 'Said that *I* deserved a night off.'

Gilmir smiled back at the odd pair, his gaze lingering on Chris's smile. What a wonderful smile that was.

Out in the main room, he saw Ada placing the two empty mugs on the bar. Coming up beside her, he rested his elbows on the counter. 'How are you?'

'Been better. And worse.' Ada turned to him with a tired smile on her face.

'I am sorry about Rayn.'

'Yeah, thanks.'

They were silent for a few moments, trying to make contact with the barkeeper who was having a busy day.

'Was it Zekatar's doing that you came to the throne room?' Gilmir broke the silence.

'No. I mean … I don't know ... I spoke to him in the cell. I reached out and found him. He told me how to get out, I think.'

'I see,' Gilmir said. 'Did he tell you to go to the throne room also?'

'No, I don't think so. Why?'

'I just realised he has been pulling the strings for a long while. I was wondering how far his reach was.'

'Okay. I tried reaching out to you. But I could not break through. You guard yourself closely.' Ada looked at him. Studied him.

'You did reach me. In a dream at least. I understand that now. But why did you go to the throne room?'

'A voice. But not Zekatar. And obviously not you. He told me to go. To find the shards before the demon used them for more evil.' Ada turned her gaze toward the barkeeper again.

'That does not sound good. You have to guard yourself.'

'Sorry, I was busy dying.'

'Of course. But in the future. Did he tell you to bring the shards to him?'

'No. Just to get them. Why?'

'I think there are other forces hunting the stones. Stronger forces.'

Ada sighed. 'Are you telling me—once again—that this isn't over?'

'Far from over. It—whatever this is—has barely started.'

CPSIA information can be obtained
at www.ICGtesting.com
Printed in the USA
LVHW032335071220
673554LV00020B/4181